# Dreams in the Clouds

Ethan Walsh

# Contents

# Chapter 1

Nihal, a bright boy from a humble village, had always dreamed of a life beyond his circumstances. Growing up in a poor family, he was determined to change his destiny through education. With a clever mind and a passion for hospitality, he earned top grades in junior college, securing admission to a prestigious university's hospitality program along with a scholarship.

Excitement bubbled within him as he traveled from his village to the bustling city, marveling at the tall buildings and vibrant streets. Upon arrival, he learned that all out-of-state students were required to live on campus. Fortunately, his seat was confirmed, and a room awaited him in the university hostel.

Once settled, Nihal eagerly attended the induction session for new students. Surrounded by eager faces, he listened intently as faculty members outlined the rigorous standards of the hospitality industry. Boys were required to wear crisp white dress shirts, tailored navy blazers, dark trousers, and polished black shoes, along with name badges. The grooming standards emphasized the importance of presentation, with boys needing to be clean-shaven and neatly groomed.

For the girls, the uniform consisted of tailored white blouses and knee-length skirts, also with blazers. They were to wear closed-toe shoes and could accessorize with light makeup and pearl earrings, their hair styled in neat buns.

Nihal felt a twinge of apprehension; he had grown his hair long since high school, embracing a personal passion he wasn't ready to abandon. Determined to honor his individuality while adhering to the standards, he approached the administrative office. His request to keep his long hair was swiftly declined, but the administrator explained that he could seek permission from the principal.

Meeting the principal made Nihal nervous, but as he shared his story—his struggles and academic achievements—he saw understanding in her eyes. After some deliberation, she proposed a compromise: if he could style his long hair into a bun, he could keep it. Grateful, Nihal agreed.

The next morning, he styled his hair into a neat bun and donned his crisp uniform. As he entered the classroom, excitement and nerves surged within him. Some students glanced at him mischievously, while others appeared genuinely intrigued. Nihal took a deep breath, settled into the front row, and prepared to immerse himself in the world of hospitality.

His first day was filled with introductions to the curriculum and his new classmates, setting the stage for a transformative journey. Little did he know that this was just the beginning of a path that would challenge and inspire him, helping him carve his own identity in the hospitality industry.

As Nihal settled into university life, he quickly realized that the journey ahead would be filled with both challenges and opportunities. With his unique background and aspirations, he was determined to make the most of his experience, forging friendships and embracing the lessons that lay ahead. Little did he know, his story was just beginning, and the path to his dreams would lead him to unexpected places.

# Chapter 2

S HALINI – "was the embodiment of grace and charm at the college. With her long, flowing hair and warm smile, she easily captured the hearts of her peers. Raised in a supportive family that valued education and kindness, Shalini excelled academically while also being involved in various extracurricular activities. Her genuine nature and ability to connect with others made her a beloved figure on campus. As the daughter of a respected professor, she often felt the weight of expectations, but her down-to-earth personality kept her grounded. Shalini's friendship with Nihal ignited a spark within her, leading her to explore deeper emotions she had never felt before.

NEEL - on the other hand, was the quintessential rich kid—the son of a successful businessman with a flair for the dramatic. With striking features and an enviable confidence, he was used to getting his way. His background afforded him the best of everything, from private tutors to exclusive social events, shaping him into a charismatic but somewhat arrogant individual. While he excelled in academics and sports, Neel's attitude often rubbed others the wrong way. His infatuation with Shalini only fueled his competitiveness, particularly when he saw her with Nihal. Determined to win her heart, Neel resorted to cunning strategies to undermine his rival, showcasing a darker side to his otherwise polished exterior.

Together, Shalini and Neel represented two different worlds within the collegge.

- one driven by genuine connection and the...
- other by privilege and ambition—setting the stage for an intense rivalry.

In the vibrant world of college life, Nihal found himself immersed in the dynamic realm of hospitality. With each passing day, he soaked up the knowledge of etiquette and manners, quickly mastering the art of charm and charisma. His participation in every class activity and sport showcased his multifaceted talents, making him a beloved figure among his peers. As weeks turned into months, Nihal's affable nature and clever wit won him a diverse group of friends, solidifying his reputation as a charismatic leader on campus.

Amidst this whirlwind of social interactions, he encountered Shalini—a stunningly beautiful girl who captured the attention of every boy in college. Unlike others who fawned over her, Nihal treated her as an equal, without the pretense that often accompanied admiration. This genuine approach intrigued Shalini; she saw something in Nihal that set him apart from the rest. As they spent more time together, sharing laughs and lighthearted moments, Shalini found herself drawn to him in ways she hadn't anticipated.

Their connection deepened, culminating in a defining moment in the assembly hall when Shalini bravely confessed her feelings for Nihal. To her delight, he reciprocated, and their relationship blossomed, making them the talk of the campus. Their popularity surged, but with fame came complications.

Enter Neel, the quintessential antagonist of their story. With his striking looks and undeniable talent, Neel was a force to be reckoned with—handsome and confident, he had always been the center of attention. For years, he harbored a secret crush on Shalini, and now, seeing her with Nihal ignited a fierce rivalry within him. Neel couldn't bear the thought of losing Shalini to someone he considered inferior.

Determined to reclaim his throne, Neel began to undermine Nihal at every opportunity. Whether through competitive college activities or subtle sabotage, Neel's efforts were relentless. He played the field skillfully, often besting Nihal in various competitions, which earned him accolades and the favor of the faculty. Meanwhile, Nihal, buoyed by his innate charm and the support of his friends, managed to win the heart of the principal, further entrenching the rivalry.

As the semester progressed, the tension between Nihal and Neel escalated. Each event became a battleground, a test of skills and resolve. Nihal's consistent performance in academics and hospitality began to earn him respect, but Neel's swagger and charisma kept him in the spotlight. Friends were divided, and the atmosphere on campus grew electric with gossip and speculation about who would come out on top.

The stakes were raised when a prestigious inter-college competition was announced, pitting them against each other in a series of challenges that would test not just their talents but also their character. With Shalini caught in the middle, the upcoming events promised to be not just a clash of skill, but also a battle for her heart.

# Chapter 3

As months passed, the tension between Nihal and Shalini blossomed into a playful camaraderie. They spent countless hours together, crafting memories filled with laughter. Shalini often played with Nihal's long hair, experimenting with different hairstyles, which only deepened their bond amidst the lively chaos of college life.

When the college announced the annual function, excitement buzzed across campus. The principal revealed that this year's event would be special, with a grand scale unlike anything seen before. They needed 20 talented volunteers to welcome celebrity guests from the hospitality and related industries. The announcement sent ripples of enthusiasm through the student body, prompting many to apply.

After a competitive audition process, Shalini secured her spot among the ten selected girls. In the boys' category, nine were chosen, but the faculty faced a dilemma between Nihal and Neel, both strong candidates who had applied at the last moment. Neel was favored by the faculty for his charisma, while Nihal had the principal's support for his creativity and stage presence. After some debate, the faculty decided to select both boys, much to everyone's relief. They also announced that since they were inviting 20 guests, they would have an extra volunteer-meaning one of the boys would host the event.

Eager to take on the hosting role, both Nihal and Neel engaged in friendly banter and a bit of playful competition. "May the best man win," Nihal teased with a smirk.

"Don't get too cocky, Nihal. I've got a few tricks up my sleeve," Neel shot back with a wink.

As preparations began, everyone immersed themselves in rehearsals. Nihal joined Shalini after his boys' group sessions, and despite the girls initially being secretive about their dance, Shalini managed to persuade them to let Nihal watch. The girls' performance, rooted in classical dance, was exquisite, and Nihal found himself mesmerized not just by the art but by Shalini's grace and confidence.

"Wow, Shalini, you're going to steal the show!" he exclaimed one day after a particularly stunning rehearsal. Shalini blushed, her cheeks turning a delicate shade of pink.

"You think so? I might need a handsome partner to match my skills," she flirted back, her eyes sparkling with mischief.

Nihal grinned. "Well, if you need a partner, I guess I could be convinced to step in. Just promise not to step on my toes!"

Their playful banter continued as the event approached, building an electric atmosphere around them. With only two days left until the annual event, the faculty checked in on everyone's preparations. All declared they were ready-except for Nihal, who had been sneakily practicing his hosting lines with Shalini.

During their rehearsal for the couple dance, Nihal and Shalini found themselves in a rhythm that felt both exhilarating and intimate. As they practiced their steps, Shalini playfully spun away, only to be gently pulled back into Nihal's embrace. The atmosphere was charged with energy as they laughed, their eyes sparkling with shared excitement.

"Careful, or you might sweep me off my feet," Shalini teased, her heart racing as Nihal leaned in closer.

"That's the plan," he replied, a mischievous grin on his face.

With each twirl and dip, they lost themselves in the moment, their connection deepening with every move. As the music swelled, Nihal dipped Shalini dramatically, holding her close. In that fleeting moment, caught up in the magic of their practice, he leaned down and brushed his lips against hers-a soft, lingering kiss that sent butterflies fluttering in both their stomachs.

Shalini blushed, her breath hitching. "Wow, that was unexpected," she said, a shy smile spreading across her face.

Nihal chuckled, his eyes gleaming. "Just getting into character. Besides, you make it hard to resist."

As they continued rehearsing, they began to discuss their performance for the event day. With excitement in their voices, they decided that they would end their dance with a kiss, making it a grand moment that would capture the audience's heart.

"Let's make it unforgettable," Nihal suggested, a hint of mischief in his tone.

Shalini nodded, her eyes sparkling with anticipation. "Definitely. A perfect way to seal the performance."

With their plan in place, they resumed their rehearsal, the kiss adding a new layer of chemistry to their performance. Both felt the thrill of what was yet to come on stage, eager to share that special moment with everyone.

"Ready to wow the crowd?" Shalini asked, a teasing lilt in her voice.

"Only if I have the most beautiful girl by my side," Nihal replied, his tone playful yet sincere.

As the final rehearsals loomed, the energy on campus was palpable, filled with excitement, anticipation, and the unmistakable chemistry brewing between Nihal and Shalini. They were ready to shine together, whatever role they would play on that grand night.

# Chapter 4

As the annual day approached, excitement buzzed through the college halls. Nine couples were fine-tuning their performances, while the boys and girls practiced their group dances. Everyone assumed that Nihal and Shalini would perform as the tenth couple, a role seemingly destined for them. Neel, with a resigned expression, was set to host the show, muttering about his bad luck. Little did anyone know, fate had other plans.

One afternoon, the faculty summoned Neel, Nihal, and Shalini to the principal's office. A heavy tension hung in the air as they entered the cabin. The principal, a strong-willed woman known for her no-nonsense attitude, sat with a serious expression, flanked by several faculty members.

"Nihal, could you step outside for a moment?" she instructed, her tone leaving no room for argument. Confusion washed over Nihal as he waited, heart racing with anxiety. When Neel and Shalini finally emerged, Neel wore a smug grin, while Shalini's expression was a mix of concern and disappointment.

"What happened?" Nihal asked, concern evident in his voice.

Shalini sighed, her brow furrowed. "The principal wants to speak with you. It's serious."

Steeling himself, Nihal stepped into the office, where the atmosphere felt thick with urgency. The principal's stern gaze met his, and he could sense that something was amiss.

"Nihal, we have an urgent situation," she began, her voice firm. "This event is critical for our college's reputation, especially with top personalities in attendance. Unfortunately, the girl assigned to escort the chief guest was in an accident this morning. We need you to step in."

Nihal's eyes widened in disbelief. "Are you kidding? I can't do that. I'm not a girl!"

The principal held her ground. "Neel is too masculine for this role, and you have certain feminine traits that would allow you to pass. Plus, your long hair works in your favor. You already know the event and can coordinate easily. We have professionals to assist with your transformation."

"Sorry, I can't do that," Nihal protested, shaking his head.

The principal leaned in, her voice lowering. "If you refuse, we'll have to cancel your scholarship. If you agree, we can offer you free education for a year. The choice is yours. You have five minutes."

Nihal's heart sank. Coming from a poor background, he couldn't risk losing his scholarship. He felt cornered and defeated. With a heavy sigh, he finally relented. "Fine. I'll do it."

"Great. Meet with the faculty and prepare," she said, her demeanor softening slightly.

As Nihal left the office, he found Shalini waiting for him. Neel lingered nearby, a smirk playing on his lips.

"What's going on?" Shalini asked, her eyes searching Nihal's face for answers.

Nihal explained the situation, and Shalini offered a supportive smile. "You won't be alone in this. I'll help you prepare."

With Shalini's encouragement, Nihal met with the faculty, who laid out an extensive plan. He would need to learn the steps for the girls' group dance, and Shalini eagerly volunteered to teach him. However, another twist awaited them: the faculty revealed that the ideal couple would perform a routine that included a kiss, a detail Shalini immediately balked at.

"What do you mean you won't do it?" Nihal asked, incredulous.

"The faculty wants the last performance to include a kiss, but I'm not kissing Neel!" Shalini insisted, crossing her arms defiantly.

Nihal turned to the faculty, confusion and disbelief mixing in his expression. "Is that really necessary?"

They nodded, explaining, "The last performance is meant to be the highlight of the evening, and we believe the kiss adds an emotional touch. But Shalini has opted out, so you'll need to partner with Neel instead."

Laughter erupted from Neel, who leaned against the wall with a grin. "Looks like you're stuck with me, sweetheart."

Nihal felt a surge of frustration. "No way! I'm not kissing him!"

The faculty remained firm. "You don't have a choice. The performance is in two days, and you both need to start rehearsing immediately."

Nihal exchanged exasperated glances with Neel, while Shalini stepped in, determined to support her friend. "We'll figure this out together. Focus on the dance first; we'll tackle the kiss later."

With Shalini guiding them, they dove into the choreography. Days flew by as they practiced, the tension between Nihal and Neel simmering. Neel's playful teasing made it difficult for Nihal to concentrate, and the looming kiss was a constant source of anxiety.

One evening, during a particularly challenging rehearsal, Nihal stumbled during a complex spin. Neel was quick to catch him, their bodies momentarily close. Their eyes locked, and the air thickened with an unspoken connection.

"You know, this could actually work," Neel said, his voice softening. "We just need to nail the performance."

Nihal sighed, feeling a mix of frustration and apprehension. "It's not just about the dance. It's everything else. I didn't sign up for this!"

Shalini intervened, stepping between them. "Let's take a break. Nihal, remember why you're doing this. Your scholarship is on the line, and this is a chance to shine in front of important people."

Nihal nodded, taking a deep breath. The stakes were high, and despite her discomfort, she resolved to focus on the performance. They resumed practice, and as they worked together, Nihal began to adapt to the rhythm.

As the event approached, the trio formed a tight bond over late-night rehearsals and shared anxieties. Nihal discovered unexpected strengths within herself, and even Neel showed glimpses of depth beneath his teasing exterior.

The night before the event, nerves ran high. Nihal sat on her bed, staring at her reflection in the mirror. The transformation process would begin early the next morning, and she felt a mix of dread and anticipation. Would she be able to pull this off?

Shalini knocked gently on the door, entering with a warm smile. "Ready for tomorrow? It's going to be amazing."

Nihal managed a weak smile. "I'm scared, Shalini. What if I mess up?"

"You won't. You've worked too hard for that. Just remember, you're not alone. We'll get through this together."

As they talked, Nihal felt her resolve strengthen. She was stepping into the unknown, but with friends by her side, maybe it wouldn't be so daunting after all.

# Chapter 5

On the morning of the event, Nihal woke up early, his heart racing with anticipation. He quickly got ready and, with excitement bubbling within him, made his way to the auditorium. As he entered, the atmosphere buzzed with energy; performers were rehearsing, and faculty members were bustling around. Taking a deep breath, Nihal stepped further inside, ready to embrace the day ahead.

As Nihal entered the transformation room, a whirlwind of activity surrounded him. Makeup artists greeted him with bright smiles, their excitement palpable. They began by cleansing his skin including waxing his body , preparing his face for the layers of makeup to come. A flawless foundation was applied, evening out her complexion, followed by delicate contouring that accentuated her cheekbones.

His eyes became the focal point as they applied shimmering eyeshadow in shades of gold and bronze, enhancing the depth of his gaze. Long, fluttery lashes were added, giving him a captivating allure. A hint of blush brought warmth to his cheeks, and finally, a bold lipstick in a rich crimson finished the look, drawing attention to his smile.

Meanwhile, a hairstylist worked diligently, weaving his long hair into soft, romantic waves that cascaded down his shoulders. A few delicate braids were intertwined, adding an element of elegance. As the final touch, a sparkling hairpin was nestled into the waves, catching the light and giving him an ethereal look.

In the fitting area, costume designers presented him with a stunning dress that shimmered under the lights. The fabric, a luxurious deep blue, hugged her figure perfectly while flowing gracefully to the floor.

To enhance his silhouette, they expertly fitted her with a padded bra and additional padding, creating curves that emphasized his newfound femininity. Intricate embroidery adorned the bodice, adding a touch of sophistication.

When she looked in the mirror, the reflection staring back was a vision of beauty and grace-a stark contrast to his usual self. Nihal felt a surge of confidence; she was ready to step into his new role, transformed both inside and out.

As the principal arrived at the auditorium, her eyes scanned the bustling scene before settling on Nihal. She paused, stunned by his transformation and the effort put into his appearance. A broad smile broke across her face as she approached him. "You look absolutely amazing, Nihal! From now on, you'll be known as Niharika for the duration of the event," she declared, handing him a name badge with "Niharika" elegantly printed on it. "Wear this proudly; it signifies your new role and the hard work you've put in." Nihal accepted the badge, feeling a rush of excitement and empowerment as he embraced his new identity for the day.........

As the venue filled with eager attendees, the atmosphere buzzed with excitement. Volunteers and faculty members directed guests to their seats while celebrity attendees began arriving in style. Among them was Miss Sanjana Mathur, the MD of Air India, whose reputation for excellence preceded her. Her presence commanded attention, and whispers of admiration filled the air.

•Attire When Escorting the Chief Guest-

•Costume:A floor-length, elegant anarkali suit in deep royal blue with intricate gold embroidery. The anarkali has a fitted bodice and flared skirt that creates a regal silhouette.

•Hairstyle:A sleek low bun adorned with fresh jasmine flowers, enhancing the traditional vibe.

•Makeup: Soft, dewy foundation with a hint of shimmer. Bold winged eyeliner and a classic red lip add a striking touch. A touch of highlighter on the cheekbones completes the look.

Niharika stood backstage, heart racing, as she prepared to escort the chief guest. When Miss Mathur arrived, Niharika greeted her with a warm smile. "It's an honor to have you here, Miss Mathur," she managed, her voice skillfully adjusted to a higher pitch, just as she practiced the day before. The two engaged in light chitchat as Niharika guided her to her seat, feeling a mixture of pride and nerves as she embraced her new role.

The event kicked off with thunderous applause, and the principal welcomed everyone with an inspiring speech, emphasizing the importance of talent and teamwork. The agenda featured an array of performances: couples dances, a fashion show, and a grand ramp walk that showcased the creativity of the students.

The spotlight soon turned to the fashion show, where Niharika and Neel took center stage. This time, Niharika wore a stunning deep pink gown that flowed gracefully with her every step, complemented by cascading curls that framed her face. They executed their walk with confidence, Niharika managing her costume effortlessly, her movements fluid and elegant. The audience was captivated by their chemistry as they strided down the runway, showcasing their ensemble.

The couples' performances began, each pair displaying unique choreography and passion.

Next, the boys took the stage with an energetic group performance that had everyone cheering.

The girls followed with a classical dance performance that highlighted their grace and precision. Dressed in exquisite silk sarees adorned with traditional embellishments, Niharika and Shalini executed their movements flawlessly.

Shalini's attire was a striking green with golden accents,

While Niharika in vibrant lehenga choli in shades of red and green, embellished with mirror work and traditional motifs. The lehenga features a flared design for ease of movement with Loose, cascading waves with a side braid decorated with small, colorful flowers and her makeup is Natural base with a focus on the eyes-smoky eye shadow and kohl for drama. Lips can be a soft pink or peach, keeping the look fresh and vibrant, enhancing their classical look.

As they danced, their expressions radiated joy and confidence, transporting the audience into a world of elegance and tradition. The choreography, filled with intricate footwork and graceful gestures, earned thunderous applause. Niharika couldn't help but notice Neel's enthusiastic reaction from the side of the stage, his eyes sparkling with admiration. "You look stunning, Niharika!" he called out, a teasing smile on his face. "I might just have to fight off a few admirers after this!"

Blushing, Niharika shot him a playful glare, trying to focus on the performance while feeling a flutter of excitement from his healthy flirting.

As the event reached its climax, it was time for the ideal couple performance. Niharika and Neel stood backstage, the energy electric. Their routine required a kiss, and although nerves tinged the air, they exchanged reassuring smiles. When they stepped onto the stage, the audience's excitement was palpable.

The music swelled, and they danced with captivating elegance. Niharika, dressed in Showcasing - A chic, fitted knee-length dress in shimmering elegant blue with a flowy overlay, adding elegance and fluidity to her movements with Half-up, half-down hairstyle with soft curls, secured with a delicate sparkly hairpin.And Glowing skin with a luminous finish, subtle contouring, and a bold berry lip. Add a hint of glitter on the eyelids for a playful yet sophisticated look.

These attires will showcase Niharika's beauty and versatility across her performances!

Felt the adrenaline rush as they executed their final moves. When the moment for the kiss arrived, Neel leaned in, planting a deep kiss that ignited cheers from the crowd. Niharika responded wholeheartedly, caught up in the performance and the thrill of the moment.

The audience erupted in applause, the guests visibly impressed by their chemistry. Shalini watched from the side, her eyes wide with surprise and delight, feeling a mix of pride and joy for her friend's success. "You nailed it!" she whispered to herself, unable to contain her excitement.

As Niharika and Neel took their final bow, the crowd continued to cheer, celebrating not just the performance but the bond that had formed between them through the ordeal. The event had been a resounding success, and for Niharika, it was a day she would never forget, filled with unexpected twists, newfound confidence, and the thrill of stepping into the spotlight.

# Chapter 6

As the event neared its exhilarating conclusion, the faculty announced that the audience would have the opportunity to select one boy and one girl as winners based on their performances. Gasps filled the room when the prizes were revealed: the boy winner would receive a tour of the industry along with his dream job, while the girl winner would embark on a fairy tale trip to Disneyland and meet supermodels at the upcoming Miss World event. Excitement buzzed through the crowd, and anticipation was palpable.

Among the boys, it was clear that Neel would take home the title, having outperformed his peers without any serious competition. The attention soon shifted to the girls, with everyone rooting for Shalini, whose grace and talent had captured hearts. But to everyone's astonishment, the name called was not Shalini's—it was Niharika, a girl known for her stunning beauty and undeniable talent. The audience erupted in applause, but confusion clouded Nihal's face as he processed the twist of fate: he had just won as a girl.

Shalini, filled with pride for her friend, quickly stepped in to guide Niharika toward the stage. "You deserve this, Nihal," she whispered encouragingly, her eyes shining with happiness for him. As they approached the winners' stand, Neel basked in his well-earned trophies and accolades. The crowd cheered for Niharika as she stepped forward, still reeling from the shock.

When Niharika reached the chief guest, Miss Sanjana, her heart raced with a mix of exhilaration and disbelief. She took a deep breath, preparing to accept her prize. But just as she did, Miss Sanjana took the microphone again, her voice firm yet compassionate. "I'm thoroughly impressed by Niharika's talent and dedication," she declared. "Not only will she receive her prize, but I'm also offering her a free scholarship for a cabin crew course, complete with air hostess training and all expenses paid. Additionally, I'd like to appoint her as our brand ambassador, with a lavish apartment and a luxurious lifestyle included."

The room fell silent, every eye glued to Niharika. She felt her heart race and her mind swirl. "I can't... how is this happening?" she murmured, the gravity of the moment almost too much to bear. Shalini squeezed her hand, offering silent support, but Nihal—now Niharika—felt as if he was losing his grip on reality.

Reality struck when he realized that the principal had already accepted Miss Sanjana's offer on his behalf, leaving him stunned in the spotlight, caught between dreams and the overwhelming weight of expectation. As he stood there, the cheers of the audience blurred into a distant hum. Niharika was not just a name anymore; it was a persona he had to embody, a life that was now expected of him.

In the crowd, Shalini beamed with joy for her friend, her heart swelling with pride. "You can do this, Nihal," she encouraged, her voice cutting through the noise. "You have always been talented and hardworking. This is your moment!" Her faith reignited a spark within him.

Niharika took a deep breath, letting Shalini's words sink in. The pressure was immense, but he realized this could be a chance for a new beginning. With shaky steps, he accepted the awards, feeling the warmth of the applause wash over him. This was a pivotal moment—not just for the girl he was named after, but for the boy who had always harbored dreams of success beyond the confines of expectation.

As the night continued, Niharika stood on stage, the future suddenly bright with possibilities. With Shalini by his side, he felt a new sense of determination blossoming within him. Perhaps this unexpected twist was the start of something truly extraordinary—a journey that could lead him to discover who he really was, both onstage and off.

As Shalini prepared to leave, the atmosphere grew charged with emotion. She leaned in, planting a soft, lingering kiss on Nihal's lips, leaving him momentarily breathless. "I'll see you soon," she whispered before turning to go, her smile still lingering in his mind.

Nihal, still in Niharika's outfit, stepped toward the changing room, trying to collect his thoughts. Suddenly, a hand pulled him into a dimly lit corner, and he froze. It was Neel, his expression serious and urgent. "I need to tell you something," he said, his voice low and intense. "I've developed feelings for Niharika. After everything we've shared, I want to be with you."

Caught off guard, Nihal hesitated. But as Neel stepped closer, the tension between them became palpable. Before Nihal could respond, Neel leaned in, capturing his lips in a kiss that sent shockwaves through him. The world around them faded as the kiss deepened, igniting a spark that Nihal hadn't expected.

In that moment, he felt a whirlwind of emotions—confusion, exhilaration, and a strange sense of acceptance. Memories of Shalini's kiss intertwined with this new experience, creating a complex tapestry of feelings. Neel's presence was both commanding and comforting, and Nihal felt himself drawn in, his heart racing.

As Neel pulled back slightly, his eyes searched Nihal's, filled with longing and vulnerability. Nihal's breath quickened, caught between the boy he was and the girl he had become. In this moment of uncertainty, he realized that perhaps this unexpected connection was leading him to discover parts of himself he had never fully embraced.

The thrill of the unknown hung in the air, leaving them both on the precipice of something profound As Tension increasing between them neel started to kiss her neck giving her love bites feeling this new sensation nihal can't help but he began to being submissive as Niharika,

Her body unknowingly responding in positive way as getting this excited neel put her hand under his hands realizing the size of his )... She mumbled fuck its huge a twice than mine.... Started shaking it soon tempting to reality Neel removed his pants and push down Niharika as he telling her to kneel down... In buzzle of excitement she kneel down and surprisingly looking at Neels)..

Started to care him,with a gentle kiss placed by her soft lips made Neel to be in heaven as going with flow Niharika took it in her mouth caring it with her toung slowly and soon she started sucking his ) like Vaccume cleaner as its her first time with her new found.. Knowing the pleasure of her efforts Neel Moaned Your perfect Baby.. Too good!!... Its the bestest one i ever get...

His moans make her excited as she going down n down... Getting the increasing cherishma He looses her tied hair and with her long hair rolling around his hand...he made stable grip over her head and pushing it down.. started drilling her mouth like drill machine...choking her throat...she Mumble's in melodious tone ummm i can't breath babe... Please slow down

Hearing that he slowdown make her relief as she started to breath again....angain he drilled like bullet train and he exclaimed Baby its coming iam about to done.. By Cumming he filled her mouth with love he didn't put out his thing as he wants her to drink it...as soon as she got the its salty taste and smirky smell she glup it down through her throat...

My Kiddo's are sliding down... A health flirting by him in playful banter ... Admiring it she stand up cleaning her face with tissues.. She tied her hairs again he planted a com-plimentary kiss on her cheek.. She left the place silently as she realized what she did.....by walking each step with blank mind she can hear his voice from behind he exclaiming...we will meet again sweetheart, i want to explore every inch of u...

as she leaving the place..

Niharika found herself in uncharted territory, grappling with the whirlwind of emotions that came with her new reality. The thrill of her secret relationship filled her with excitement, but it also cast a shadow of anxiety. Juggling her feelings for her new boyfriend while managing her past relationship with Shalini as Nihal, It was no small feat. Each day brought fresh challenges, and Niharika knew she had to navigate this delicate balance with care. Embracing her new experiences, she steeled herself to face whatever came next, determined to keep her secrets safe while nurturing the connections that mattered most.

# Chapter 7

As soon as Niharika, a new persona, stepped into the changing room, Nihal reached the hostel, greeted by congratulations from everyone. He entered his room, closed the door, and sat in a mix of excitement and confusion.

After a refreshing bath, he relaxed and called Shalini. Their conversation flowed easily, filled with laughter and shared experiences about the recent event. However, as he ended the call and tried to sleep, his mind wandered to the kiss he shared with Shalini. But as he leaned in, her face morphed into Neel's, and he was haunted by memories of their unexpected moment. Throughout the night, he dreamt of quality time with Neel, which left him unsettled.

The next morning, Nihal awoke, determined to push aside his conflicting feelings. After a fresh shower, he dressed for college, feeling a shift in how everyone perceived him. When he met with friends, the atmosphere was electric with new possibilities. Suddenly, the principal called him to her office. She congratulated him on a new opportunity, but he expressed his frustration about her signing a contract with an airline without his consent.

Noticing his anger, she calmly offered him a glass of water, employing her persuasive skills. "This is crucial for both you and our university," she explained. "You have a bright future ahead as Niharika. Don't miss this chance." She sweetened the deal by promising special rewards-a scholarship for his training and a mentorship with industry professionals.

"By clearing this semester, you'll be headed for aviation training as a cabin crew member for six months. After that, you'll have an opportunity to work with Miss Sanjana's airline, contingent on your interview performance."........

Curious, Nihal asked why certain documents were necessary. The principal clarified, "You will be training as Niharika, so we need everything in order. From tomorrow, I will personally oversee your physical training."

"What do you mean?" he asked, a mix of curiosity and apprehension in his voice.

"Air hostesses need to maintain a perfect figure," she said with a smile. "I've hired a yoga instructor and a gym trainer, along with a specialized diet plan. Everything is sponsored. You'll start your new routine tomorrow."

Reluctantly, he agreed. After joining his classes, he excitedly shared the news with Shalini, who was thrilled for him and delighted to have a new best friend in his life.

The day ended, and Nihal awoke early the next morning for his first yoga session with Miss Jenny. She was an experienced instructor, her presence calm and encouraging. "Welcome, Niharika. Over the next month, we will focus on developing flexibility, strength, and balance," she explained. "Each session will include various poses designed to enhance your core and improve your posture-both essential for your future career."

They began with deep breathing exercises, followed by a series of stretches that made his body feel alive. Miss Jenny guided him through sun salutations, emphasizing the importance of alignment and mindfulness.

Later, he met Miss Richa, his new gym trainer and dietitian. With a warm smile, she laid out a rigorous gym routine. "We'll be focusing on overall fitness and toning your body to meet the airline's criteria. Expect strength training, cardio, and core workouts designed to enhance your natural curves."

She handed him a carefully crafted meal plan, rich in proteins, healthy fats, and vibrant fruits and vegetables. "This diet will fuel your workouts and help you achieve a healthy, fit body," she assured him.

As Nihal continued to embrace his new identity as Niharika, he committed fully to his daily routine. Each morning began with yoga sessions led by Miss Jenny, enhancing his flexibility and balance. Afterward, he pushed himself in the gym with Miss Richa, whose tailored workouts were sculpting his physique. She had even given him a special cream for his chest, instructing him to use it daily, which he did without realizing the significant impact it would have.

One afternoon, after a particularly challenging workout, Nihal decided to consult Miss Richa. "I've noticed changes in my chest. Is that normal?" he asked, a hint of uncertainty in his voice.

She smiled knowingly. "It's part of your transformation, Niharika. The cream is working wonders for you."

Feeling both excited and apprehensive, he sought out the principal for further clarity. During their meeting, she encouraged him to wear a supportive bra to help shape his silhouette. "It's all part of your journey," she assured him, and he reluctantly agreed to give it a try.

Eager to share his experiences, Nihal turned to Shalini, who quickly became his confidante. "So, how's the transformation going?" she asked one day, her eyes sparkling with curiosity.

"It's intense! I feel different, especially with my body," he admitted, his cheeks flushing.

Shalini grinned, leaning closer. "Different how? Are you finally embracing those curves?"

"Let's just say my chest is starting to look... more feminine," he confessed, feeling a mix of pride and embarrassment.

"Awesome! We need to celebrate!" she exclaimed. "How about a trip to the beauty parlor this weekend? I'll help you with all the girly stuff!"

Nihal agreed, excited yet nervous about the upcoming day. When Saturday arrived, they stepped into the parlor, where the air was fragrant with lavender and the soft sounds of music played in the background.

Shalini immediately took charge. "Alright, Niharika, first things first-let's work on that skin!" She led him to a treatment chair where a friendly aesthetician, Maya, welcomed them.

"Welcome, Niharika! Ready for some pampering?" Maya asked, her smile bright.

As Maya started applying a soothing mask to Nihal's face, Shalini leaned in. "This is going to make your skin glow," she whispered. "Just wait until the guys see you!"

Nihal chuckled, feeling slightly self-conscious but also flattered. "You think I'll attract attention?"

"Absolutely! With the right makeup, you'll be turning heads," she teased, giving him a playful nudge.

After the facial, they moved to hair treatments. Shalini insisted on trying a new hairstyle that would highlight his long hair. "Let's add some waves! It'll look so cute!" she declared.

As the stylist worked, Shalini and Nihal shared gossip and laughter. She demonstrated how to create playful curls using a curling iron. "See? Like this!" she said, expertly curling a lock of her own hair. "Just hold it for a few seconds, and voilà!"

"Okay, but how do you not burn your fingers?" Nihal asked, feigning exasperation.

"It's all in the technique!" she laughed, showing him how to wrap the hair without getting too close to the iron.

After the hair session, they headed to the makeup area. Shalini took charge again, pulling out various palettes. "Let's play! I want to show you how to enhance those cheekbones," she said, applying blush with precision.

As she worked, Shalini leaned in, her face inches from his. "You know, you're really pulling this off, Niharika. I'm so proud of you," she said softly, her eyes sparkling.

Feeling a flutter in his stomach, Nihal smiled back. "Thanks, Shalini. I couldn't have done this without your support."

"Now, for the final touch-lip color!" she exclaimed, selecting a soft pink shade. "This will make your smile pop."

As she applied the lipstick, their eyes met, and for a moment, the air was charged with something more than friendship. Nihal felt his heart race as Shalini playfully smudged some lipstick on the corner of his mouth. "Oops! Looks like I've got some on you!" she laughed, wiping it away with her finger, lingering a moment too long.

After their beauty session, they stepped outside, the sun shining brightly. Shalini turned to him, her expression sincere. "You look amazing, Niharika. Seriously. I can't believe how far you've come."

"Thanks! I feel... different," he said, glancing down at his reflection in a shop window. The changes in his chest were more pronounced, and he felt a sense of pride in his appearance.

"By the way," Shalini added with a mischievous grin, "if you need a bra, I have a few that you can borrow. They'll fit you perfectly!"

Nihal hesitated, then replied with a playful smile, "Okay, why not? I guess I'll need one if I'm going to take this seriously."

"Great! I'll bring some over tomorrow. You'll be so stylish!" she said, winking at him.

Over lunch that day, they shared stories and dreams, and Shalini flirted playfully. "You know, with your new look, you could definitely be the star of a reality show. 'The Transformation of Niharika!'"

"Ha! I'd need a lot of drama to keep that interesting," he joked, but deep down, he relished the attention and camaraderie.

As the day came to an end, Nihal felt a deeper connection with Shalini. Their playful banter and shared experiences had drawn them closer, turning an ordinary beauty day into something truly special. Each moment spent together felt like a stepping stone toward a new beginning-not just for his transformation, but for their budding friendship.

With each passing day, Nihal embraced his new identity, finding strength in his journey and support in Shalini's unwavering friendship. He looked forward to what lay ahead, ready to face challenges with a smile and a heart full of hope.

# Chapter 8

A month and a half had passed since Nihal began his journey as Niharika. With dedication to his new routine, he had transformed his physique, meeting the criteria for cabin crew training. He felt confident and empowered in his new identity, seamlessly embracing the role.

One afternoon, the principal called him into her office. "Congratulations, Niharika," she said, handing him an envelope with a proud smile.

Curious, he opened it to find several official documents. His heart raced as he saw his new name-Niharika-printed on each one, alongside a recent photo of him in full makeup and attire. The documents included an identification card, training acceptance letter, and various certificates required in the aviation industry, like first aid training and customer service training credentials.

"This is it. You are officially Niharika now," the principal said warmly.

"Thank you so much! I really appreciate everything you've done for me," Niharika replied, beaming with pride. The principal's support had been invaluable throughout this journey.

"Next week is your semester exam, and after that, you'll be ready for training. You're going to do great things, Niharika," she encouraged.

Excited, Niharika rushed to share the news with Shalini. When she arrived at their usual meeting spot, she greeted him with an enthusiastic hug.

"Niharika! This calls for a celebration!" Shalini exclaimed, her eyes sparkling with excitement. "You're officially on your way to becoming a cabin crew member!"

As they celebrated, Shalini glanced at her playfully. "Since you've been borrowing my bra for the past three weeks, it's time we go shopping for your official ones! You need a whole new wardrobe to match your fabulous new self."

"Shopping? That sounds amazing!" Niharika replied, her heart fluttering at the thought of a fun day with Shalini.

The next day, they set off for the mall, filled with anticipation. As they walked through the bustling corridors, Shalini grabbed Niharika's hand. "First stop: lingerie! You need the best!"

They entered a chic lingerie store, where colorful bras and panties adorned the walls. Shalini picked out several styles, holding them up for Niharika to see. "What do you think of this one? It's cute and practical." she said, showing a lacy bralette.

Niharika giggled. "It's adorable! I love it."

After trying on a few pieces, Niharika felt a surge of confidence. "I can't believe I'm doing this!" she said, admiring herself in the mirror. "I feel so... different."

"You look incredible! Just wait until the boys see you," Shalini teased, winking. "You'll be turning heads everywhere!"

Next, they ventured into a trendy women's clothing store. Shalini picked out dresses, blouses, and skirts, insisting Niharika try everything on. They giggled as they squeezed into the changing rooms, trying on various outfits.

As they both changing their clothes together,we know Nihal who hinding his real identity of being man ( his manhood) under the panties

as Niharika -she saw Shalinis inner beauty made her excited as getting bonnr by her beautiful body, Shalini caught her by looking it through Niharikas Panty as soon as tension released, Shalini hugged Niharika and their Melon's pressing eachothers getting squeezed by the hug made excite both of them,

Shalini planted a genuine kiss on Niharikas soft lips as their lips met soon they liplocked , their toungs fighting with mixing the test of their lip glosses and sailiva together a passionate deep kiss ended, both started caring each others body with gentle cuddling to intense fore play,

pressing her melons Shalini made next move towards Niharikas Past secret a Smirky and masculine toy between her legs.. She started caring him with her tounge soon became sucking macine, Niharika enjoying the movement...

She going to made next move,

Niharika hold one leg of Shalini from her ankle stretching it towords sky, made Shalini lean forward and she took support of side wall to be stable....

Niharika inserts her Huge Lovely Manhood under Shalinis little rosehole

As Niharika increasing the speed, Shalini started moaning loudly ... Knowing their presence in public place Niharika put one hand of her On Shalinis mouth to maintain the silence

With increased speed and hitting her back to turning her butt Red with gentle slaps

"Niharika Took-Off Shalinis Verginity "

along with intimacy Niharika ponuding her rosehole with love and warm milky thik cream...as Niharika pull out her Manhood the cream leaked down from Shalinis Beautiful Rosehole With cleaning their self they planted one last kiss...

wear their cloths and step out through trial room... Sharing laughters both can see happiness on eachothers face...

"Let's see the next one!" Shalini encouraged as Niharika stepped out in a fitted sundress. "You look like a dream! You'll kill them with your looks!"

"Stop it! You're making me blush!" Niharika laughed, twirling in the dress.

They spent hours mixing and matching outfits, creating a full wardrobe that included:

• Dresses : Flowy maxi dresses, chic bodycon dresses, and cute sundresses.

• Tops : Stylish blouses and trendy crop tops.

• Bottoms : High-waisted jeans, stylish skirts, and tailored trousers.

• Lingerie :A variety of bras and panties, from everyday comfort to playful lace.

• Shoes :Trendy sandals, heels, and comfy flats.

• Makeup :A new collection of makeup essentials, including foundation, blush, and lip gloss.

After their shopping spree, they found a cozy café for a break. Over steaming cups of coffee, they laughed and chatted about their day. "I can't believe how much fun this was! Thank you for making me do this," Niharika said, feeling grateful for Shalini's support.

"Are you kidding? I had a blast! And you looked stunning in every outfit. I'm so proud of you!" Shalini beamed, her eyes shining with admiration.

As they finished their drinks, Shalini leaned closer, her expression softening. "You know, Niharika, I've really enjoyed spending this time with you you mean a lot to me.

Feeling a warmth spread through her, Niharika replied, "You mean so much to me too, Shalini. I couldn't have made it this far without you."

Their eyes locked for a moment, and Niharika felt a flutter in her stomach. There was a spark of something deeper, something beautiful blossoming between them.

As they walked out of the café, Shalini playfully nudged Niharika. "Let's take a selfie to remember our fabulous shopping day!" They posed together, beaming at the camera, capturing the joy of the moment.

"Ready to slay the world as Niharika balini asked, her playful spirit shining through.

"Absolutely! With you by my side, I feel unstoppable," Niharika replied, confidence radiating.

The day ended with laughter, fun, and a deeper connection forged through shared experiences. Niharika felt ready to take on the world, supported by the unwavering friendship of Shalini and the exciting journey ahead.

# Chapter 9

As dawn broke over the college campus, students buzzed with excitement, eager to collect their admit cards. Among them was Niharika, who, after a long holiday, stepped into the corridor with an elegant grace that drew admiring glances. Her stylish outfit-a fitted cream blouse paired with high-waisted navy trousers-made her stand out, radiating confidence.

Just then, a sleek, brand-new sports car glided into the parking lot, capturing everyone's attention. Niharika's heart raced as she recognized it-the very model she had always dreamed of. As the driver emerged, she was met with the warm, inviting smile of Neel. Once rivals, their relationship had taken a surprising turn, and seeing him now sparked a mixture of excitement and uncertainty in her.

Trying to mask her nervousness, she managed a playful laugh, but her heart thumped louder. Shalini, her girlfriend and closest confidante, arrived on the scene, her surprise evident as she noticed Niharika chatting with Neel. "What's going on here?" Shalini asked, a hint of disbelief in her tone.

The closeness between Niharika and Neel stirred feelings of doubt within her, memories of their past rivalry creeping back.

As they exchanged playful banter, Shalini couldn't shake the unease she felt. Were they truly friends now? Still, she joined in the laughter, determined to keep things light. Together, they made their way toward the exam hall, marking the end of their first paper. Days turned into weeks as exams continued, and despite her initial reservations, Shalini watched as their bond grew stronger. Neel had developed feelings for Niharika, but she maintained her charm and grace, keeping both of their hearts guessing.

With the semester winding down, Niharika prepared for a new chapter. In just two days, she would be flying to begin her training as a cabin crew member, a dream she had cherished for years. The college organized a grand farewell, with faculty and friends celebrating her journey ahead. Shalini helped her pack, throwing in playful jabs about how she would miss her and how she better not forget them once she became a glamorous flight attendant.

The next morning, Shalini accompanied Niharika to the airport, ready to say goodbye. As they entered the bustling terminal, they spotted Neel, who seemed equally surprised to see them. In a moment of spontaneity, he leaned in and kissed Niharika on the cheek. Niharika's cheeks flushed, and she smiled warmly in response. Shalini, caught off guard, felt a pang of uncertainty but masked it with a supportive smile.

With a heartfelt goodbye, Niharika stepped toward her dream, boarding her flight filled with hope and excitement. Upon landing, she was greeted by Miss Sanjana, the Managing Director of one of India's top airlines. Miss Sanjana had sponsored Niharika's training and appointed her as the brand ambassador for the airline, complete with a lavish apartment and a brand-new car as rewards for her hard work.

As Niharika walked through the airport corridor, a grand entry awaited her. Dressed in a stylish ensemble of a tailored blazer over a soft silk blouse and fitted trousers, she commanded attention. The atmosphere turned electric as applause erupted, dancers performed vibrant routines, and a band played uplifting music, transforming the airport into a celebratory space. Niharika's heart swelled with pride as she absorbed the warm reception.

Once the celebrations subsided, she was escorted to Miss Sanjana's lavish office. The room exuded elegance, with plush furnishings and a breathtaking view of the city skyline. "Welcome, Niharika," Miss Sanjana greeted her with a warm smile. "I'm thrilled to have you on board. Your training begins tomorrow, and I'll ensure you get extra lessons and special treatment. You've already impressed everyone here."

Niharika felt a rush of gratitude. They chatted about the airline's vision and her role as an ambassador, with Miss Sanjana

sharing insights about upcoming promotional shoots sched-
uled for weekends. "Get ready for some exciting adventures,"
she said, her eyes sparkling. "You'll be the face of our brand,
and I have big plans for you."

As they wrapped up their meeting and Paper Work , Miss
Sanjana led Niharika to her new apartment. When she entered, her breath caught in her throat-a luxurious space
that seemed almost unreal. The apartment was expansive,
adorned with modern decor and breathtaking views.

"Welcome home," a servant said, guiding her through the
opulent space. Niharika's eyes widened as she discovered her
wardrobe, already filled with designer clothes, ranging from
elegant dresses to chic casual wear. Each section was meticulously organized, showcasing everything from fashionable
outerwear to trendy accessories.

"Wow, this is incredible!" Niharika exclaimed, running her
fingers over the fabrics. There were even sections dedicated
to shoes-stilettos, sneakers, and everything in between-along
with skincare products, cosmetics, and daily essentials that
had been thoughtfully curated. It was a dream come true, and
she marveled at how quickly her life had transformed.

"This is a dream come true in the most unexpected way," she
mumbled, unable to contain her excitement. After settling in,
she took a soothing bath, indulging in her skincare routine
as she reflected on her journey. She was ready for this new
chapter of her life, and as she slipped into bed, exhaustion

washed over her. She closed her eyes, a smile playing on her lips, knowing that her adventure was just beginning.

As she drifted off to sleep, thoughts of Shalini and Neel danced in her mind, reminding her of the friendships she held dear and the challenges that lay ahead. She was ready to embrace it all.

As Niharika embarked on her exciting new journey, the challenges of her cabin crew training loomed ahead. With weekends filled with glamorous photo shoots and brand ambassador duties, she found herself navigating the complexities of her emerging career while managing her relationships with Shalini and Neel. As old rivalries threatened to resurface and new friendships blossomed, Niharika would have to confront her feelings and the dynamics between the three of them. Would she be able to balance her ambitions with the tangled emotions that came with love and friendship? The journey ahead promised growth, self-discovery, and unexpected twists, leaving readers eager to see what unfolds next.

# Chapter 10

As the morning sun spilled through the blinds of her apartment, Niharika felt a sense of anticipation. It wasn't just the thrill of starting another day at the prestigious cabin crew academy, but also the excitement of stepping further into her journey of becoming an aviation professional. She lived alone, which meant she had become fiercely independent, managing her own space and time with precision.

Her day began, as always, with a detailed skincare routine—her face glowing with confidence as she prepared for another intense day of training. Niharika selected her outfit for the day carefully: a pastel pink blouse paired with a high-waisted black pencil skirt. She let her long hair fall in soft waves over her shoulders today, projecting a blend of elegance and charm. Her attire spoke volumes about her professionalism, while her hair and minimal makeup emphasized her natural beauty.

Niharika was also living in the shadow of a secret triumph. She had already been appointed as the brand ambassador for the airline during the academy's annual day function, even before her formal training began. The management had spotted her potential — her grace, confidence, and professionalism set her apart. This role came with additional responsibility, but it filled her with pride.

• Arriving at the Academy :

Niharika arrived at the academy, where the bustling energy of trainees and staff greeted her. The grandeur of the building still managed to inspire her every morning. She had formed deep bonds with the other girls — Tanya, Ayesha, and Meera, all of whom shared her passion and determination to succeed.

Though Niharika was deeply invested in her training, she made it a point to share her experiences with Shalini, Every evening, she called Shalini to give her the day's updates — the challenges she faced, the laughs she shared with her new friends, and the small victories she celebrated. Their conversations had become a ritual, grounding Niharika as she navigated this new world of aviation.

Amidst all of this, Niharika remained vigilant about maintaining her biggest secret — Her Past Identity between her legs and the presence of Neel, her secret boyfriend. She took great care in keeping their relationship private and her past identity , ensuring no one in the academy found out about it. Niharika was cautious with her phone calls, always stepping away to secluded spots when she needed to speak with Neel as she always remembered their intimate encounter. Even her closest friends at the academy didn't know about him, as she deftly avoided any personal questions that might reveal too much. For Niharika, it was crucial that her personal and professional lives remained separate, and she was careful not to let any hints slip.

• Shoots as a Brand Ambassador :

Despite her rigorous schedule, weekends were reserved for her responsibilities as the brand ambassador. One of her most memorable photoshoots featured a collection of the airline's promotional uniforms, where Niharika's style and beauty were highlighted with every look.

In one of the shoots, she wore the signature navy-blue cabin crew uniform, paired with a vibrant silk scarf tied elegantly around her neck. Her hair was styled into a sleek chignon, exuding sophistication. The next outfit was a more casual look—a stylish trench coat for the "off-duty" crew members, her hair tied into a high ponytail, giving her a fresh, energetic appearance. Another day, she sported a glamorous red dress for the airline's premium class promotions, her hair in loose curls cascading down her back, perfectly framing her face.

Every shoot was a new experience, with different outfits and hairstyles to highlight her versatility. Whether it was sleek updos or loose waves, Niharika's beauty always took center stage, and she learned how to carry herself with poise in front of the camera.

• A Surprise Call :

One evening, after an exhausting day at the academy, Niharika was relaxing when her phone buzzed. She frowned at the unknown number. Curiosity got the better of her, and she answered the call. For a moment, there was silence on the other end.

"Niharika?" The voice was deep, familiar, and sent her heart racing. It was Neel.

Her secret boyfriend. She hadn't spoken to him in months, their relationship shrouded in secrecy due to the demands of her training and the distance that had grown between them.

"Neel? Is that really you?" she asked, a mix of surprise and excitement in her voice.

"Yeah, it's me," he replied softly. "I know it's been a while. I just wanted to hear your voice."

The two spent the next few minutes catching up, with Niharika filling him in on her hectic schedule and how much she missed talking to him. Neel, who had been busy with his own work, understood her challenges but promised to stay in touch more frequently. Their conversation was brief but filled with warmth and familiarity. It reminded Niharika of the life she had outside the academy, one that she longed to reconnect with.

As much as the call warmed her heart, Niharika made sure to maintain her cautious approach. She ended the call and carefully deleted the number from her phone, ensuring that there was no trace of their conversation. Her secret remained safe, as always.

• Grooming and Etiquette Sessions :

The grooming and etiquette sessions at the academy were among Niharika's favorite parts of the training. These sessions weren't just about looking good—they were about presenting oneself with confidence and grace, which was vital in the aviation industry.

Niharika excelled in these sessions, her natural elegance making it easy for her to stand out. She learned the art of applying makeup flawlessly within minutes, focusing on enhancing her natural features while keeping the look professional.

Her hair, which had always been one of her most striking features, was styled in a variety of ways. Some days, she sported an intricate French braid, while other days saw her hair in a sleek high bun that added an air of authority to her persona.

The instructors paid close attention to every detail—how the trainees walked, how they greeted others, and even how they maintained eye contact during conversations. The etiquette lessons were designed to ensure that they could handle passengers from all walks of life with poise. Niharika found herself improving in areas she had never considered before—like maintaining perfect posture and speaking with just the right tone of friendliness and professionalism.

One particular class focused on how to manage delicate situations on board, such as calming nervous passengers or dealing with unruly customers. Niharika learned the fine balance between firmness and empathy, a skill that would serve her well in her future career.

• Balancing Life and Training :

Despite the intensity of the training and her responsibilities as a brand ambassador, Niharika never lost sight of her personal goals. Her friendships at the academy deepened, and she found herself laughing more and more with Ayesha, Tanya, and Meera. They often discussed the lessons learned in their grooming sessions, shared tips on maintaining healthy skin, and even practiced their walk for upcoming cabin crew interviews.

Every weekend, the girls found time to relax and unwind. They would go shopping for new outfits or head to the movies, exploring the city that had now become their second home. These moments were a welcome escape from the pressure of their training, and they strengthened the bonds between them.

Niharika's connection with her secret boyfriend, Neel, also added a layer of excitement to her otherwise demanding routine. Though their relationship remained mostly on calls and texts, the secrecy added a certain thrill to their bond. She made sure that no one at the academy ever found out about Neel, keeping every detail hidden with precision.

- The Final Phase :

As Niharika approached the final months of her training, the intensity increased. The trainees were now participating in full mock flights, where they had to manage real-life scenarios, from serving passengers to dealing with simulated emergencies. Every day was a test of their skills, composure, and ability to think on their feet.

Niharika thrived in these situations. Her experiences in the grooming and etiquette sessions, coupled with the lessons from her photoshoots, had prepared her well for this. She was no longer just another trainee—she was a leader among her peers, admired for her dedication, beauty, and confidence.

Her journey was far from over, but as she stood at the brink of graduation, Niharika knew she had transformed. From her first day at the academy, uncertain and filled with nervous excitement, to now—a poised, professional young woman ready to conquer the skies.

Niharika's future was bright, and though her path would still be filled with challenges, she was more than ready for them. The sky was no longer just a dream—it was her destination.

# Chapter 11

Niharika had blossomed into the epitome of professionalism and grace by the end of her training. Her poise, impeccable grooming, and delicate etiquette made her the perfect cabin crew candidate. The final milestone before stepping into her new career was the long-anticipated interview, to be conducted by Miss Sanjana herself. As special as Niharika was to Miss Sanjana, the pressure of the interview lingered in the back of her mind.

• The Interview: A Hidden Revelation :

On the interview day, Niharika carefully chose her attire to reflect her polished professionalism. She wore a fitted ivory blouse with delicate lace sleeves, tucked into a high-waisted navy blue pencil skirt that highlighted her sleek silhouette. Paired with classic nude pumps and a gold watch, she looked every bit the part of a refined cabin crew member. Her long hair was styled into an elegant French braid, neatly swept to the side. Minimalist pearl drop earrings adorned her ears, while a subtle gold chain with a heart pendant completed her look, giving her an air of sophistication.

The interview went as smoothly as expected. Niharika answered Miss Sanjana's questions with confidence, her smile radiant and voice calm. But as the conversation was coming to a close, Miss Sanjana, with her sharp intuition, revealed that she had uncovered Niharika's biggest secret—Her True Identity...

Niharika froze, fear creeping into her heart. But Miss Sanjana, with a mischievous smile, leaned back in her chair and said, "Relax, Niharika. Your secret is safe with me, on one condition. I'll reveal that condition after you return from graduation. For now, you should know that you've impressed me immensely. Upon your return, I'll appoint you as my personal secretary."

A flood of relief washed over Niharika, though her curiosity was piqued. What was this condition? She thanked Miss Sanjana, feeling a mix of pride and uncertainty. With many thoughts racing in her mind, Niharika packed her belongings and prepared to return to college, ready for the final chapter of her academic life.

• Reunion with Shalini: A Celebration of Friendship :

As her plane touched down, Niharika was welcomed back by her best friend Shalini, who had been eagerly waiting for her. Shalini ran up to her, pulling Niharika into a tight embrace and planting a kiss on her cheek. "I missed you so much!" Shalini exclaimed, her excitement contagious. Niharika, equally thrilled, felt a surge of warmth to be back with her closest friend.

On the way to the college, the two girls chattered away, catching up on all they had missed. Niharika shared stories from her training days, the challenges she overcame, and the secrets she still had to keep. They reached the college campus, where Niharika settled into her new room in the girls' hostel, which was conveniently near Shalini's room. Their bond, stronger than ever, radiated joy as they embraced this last leg of their academic journey together.

• The Principal's Pride :

The next morning, Niharika was called into the principal's office. The principal, a graceful and authoritative woman, greeted her warmly. Dressed in a silk saree, the principal smiled as she looked at Niharika. "I'm incredibly proud of you, Niharika," she said, her eyes glowing with pride. "You've achieved so much, and I know there are even greater things waiting for you."

Niharika felt humbled by the principal's kind words. She thanked her sincerely, feeling a renewed sense of determination to finish her final semester on a high note.

• Preparations for the Gathering -

As part of the celebrations marking the last semester, the college announced a grand gathering, where students were encouraged to perform and showcase their talents. Niharika and Shalini had already planned to perform a classical dance together, something they both loved.

On the day of the performance, Niharika was adorned in a stunning turquoise blue lehenga with intricate gold embroidery. The lehenga skirt flowed gracefully as she walked, and the matching blouse featured delicate beadwork around the neckline. She accessorized the outfit with an ornate gold choker necklace encrusted with emeralds, a pair of matching jhumkas, and gold bangles that jingled softly with every movement. Her hair was styled in a loose braid, decorated with tiny jasmine flowers, and her makeup was bold yet traditional—smoky eyes, perfectly winged eyeliner, and deep red lips.

Shalini, equally striking, wore a rich purple lehenga with silver embroidery. Her hair was tied into an elegant bun adorned with silver pins, and she wore long chandelier earrings that sparkled under the lights. Together, the two of them looked like royalty, ready to take the stage.

Their classical dance performance was a blend of grace and energy. Niharika's movements were fluid, her expressions capturing the emotion of the music. The crowd was mesmerized, watching the synchronization between the two friends as they performed intricate hand gestures and swift footwork. When the performance ended, the applause was deafening.

• The Couple's Dance: A Revelation :

After their classical dance, the next performance was announced—Niharika and Neel were to perform a couple's dance. This was a surprise to many, including Shalini, who had never seen Niharika with Neel before. The secrecy around their relationship left her curious and even a bit suspicious.

For the couple's dance, Niharika changed into a breathtaking crimson gown. The dress, with its off-shoulder neckline and fitted bodice, flowed down into soft, cascading layers of fabric that shimmered under the lights. Her jewelry was simple but stunning—diamond studs in her ears and a delicate diamond bracelet on her wrist. Her hair was styled into loose, voluminous waves that framed her face, giving her a soft yet glamorous look.

As the music began, Niharika and Neel moved across the stage with fluidity and chemistry that could not be missed. Their dance was filled with romantic gestures, and the connection between them was undeniable. As the song reached its climax, Neel pulled Niharika close and planted a passionate kiss on her lips, leaving the audience in stunned silence for a moment before they erupted into cheers.

Shalini, watching from the sidelines, was left wide-eyed. Her suspicions had been confirmed—Niharika and Neel were more than just friends. But instead of feeling jealous, she felt a sense of understanding and support.

• The Confession :

After the performance, Shalini approached Niharika with a raised eyebrow and a playful smile. "So... care to explain what just happened?" she teased, nudging Niharika Who Once  her Boyfriend but now as her Bestfriend forever...

Niharika laughed, knowing she couldn't keep the truth hidden any longer. She told Shalini everything—how she had met Neel, their secret relationship, and how she had managed to keep it all hidden, even from their closest friends. She even shared the story of Miss Sanjana discovering her secret and the mysterious condition she had yet to uncover.

Shalini listened intently, and by the time Niharika finished, she smiled warmly. "I understand now," she said, hugging Niharika. "You've been through so much, and I'm happy for you. Welcome to womanhood, Niharika."

Just as their conversation ended, Neel joined them, his arm wrapped around Niharika's waist. The three of them shared a few laughs, reminiscing about the performance and their journey so far. Together, they planned a celebration for later that evening, ready to toast to love, friendship, and the exciting future ahead.

• A New Chapter Awaits - With

Niharika, Neel, and Shalini decided to celebrate together after a long-awaited reunion. The trio planned an evening full of laughter, food, and memories, unaware of the twists fate had in store for them. As they gathered under the city lights, everything seemed perfect. But hidden secrets lingered between them, threatening to unravel the night. Just as the celebration was reaching its peak, an unexpected message shook them to the core. The truth was on the verge of coming out.

# Chapter 12

The trio decided to celebrate Neel's brilliant idea with a night out at the pub. As they left college, Shalini and Niharika headed back to the hostel to get ready. Shalini, with a playful smile, suggested a striking red dress for Niharika. "Come on, babe, you have to look stunning for your boyfriend!" she teased, her eyes sparkling with mischief.

Niharika laughed, raising an eyebrow. "And what about you?"

With a wink, Shalini replied, "I'm already yours!" The two shared a lighthearted moment, their friendship strengthened by playful banter.

After getting ready, Shalini wore a sleek black dress that hugged her figure, paired with elegant heels, while her hair cascaded in soft waves.

Niharika opted for a form-fitting red dress that highlighted her curves, complemented by her hair styled in a chic updo adorned with a delicate clip.

Neel arrived in style, stepping out of an expensive luxury car. He wore a tailored navy shirt and fitted jeans, exuding confidence as he opened the door for the girls. They settled into the car, excitement bubbling in the air as they headed to the pub.

As they entered, the vibrant atmosphere was electrifying. For Niharika and Shalini, it was their first experience in such a lively setting. They quickly found themselves immersed in the rhythm of the night. Neel, effortlessly charming, flirted with Niharika, complimenting her beauty and making her blush. Shalini chimed in with playful remarks, teasing Neel about his smooth talk.

"Are you trying to win her over, or are you just that good at flirting?" Shalini laughed, nudging Niharika.

"I'm just being honest," Neel replied with a smirk, his gaze lingering on Niharika.

After a few rounds of drinks, Shalini suggested they hit the dance floor. They danced together, laughter echoing around them. In a moment of spontaneity, Neel pulled Niharika close and planted a passionate kiss on her lips, catching both of them off guard. Shalini, sensing the chemistry, playfully joined in, giving Niharika a quick peck as well.

"Looks like we're having a wild night!" Shalini exclaimed, raising her glass.

As the night wore on and the drinks flowed, Neel suggested heading back to his place. Both Niharika and Shalini agreed, their excitement palpable. They arrived at Neel's sprawling mansion, where he led them to his lavish room, adorned with modern decor and a grand bed.

"Welcome to my humble abode," he joked, gesturing around. The room radiated luxury, and the ambiance felt charged with potential.

They settled in, the chemistry between the three of them unmistakable. With laughter and flirtation in the air, they started with cuddles becoming foreplay and Niharika being submissive...

Both Shalini and Neel getting  advantage of it...they both started exploring Niharikas body as soon as they complete their intense foreplay the trio was totally naked admiring eachothers body with healty teasing Neel Exclaimed wow they are perfectly grown looking at Niharikas Perfect round shaped Boobies with a pale pinkish brown areolas around her highlighted button sized nipples.. Neel started to lick them while Shalini started with Niharikas Dick caring with her mouth and shaking Neels Dick with her another hand... Increasing tension of intimacy between them..

Niharika hold Shalini on side table she put her Dick inside shalinis Pink Rosehole by stretching her legs to the opposite direction making her moan...

As getting excited by the scene Neel joins them from Niharikas Back side as he pushing Niharika Forward And spredind her ass using his both hands...

He spits on Niharikas Amazingly Beautiful Shaved asshole with her Bubbles smooth butt as its inviting Neel inn....He hold Niharika By her Waist and inserted his Dick slowly...as Its very huge Niharika exclaimed Baby its huge go slowly....

He started to fuck Niharika who fuking Shalini... The trio enjoying the movement of Threesome's both Niharika And Neel pounded the gaps inbetween with their love and creamy white thik liquid as intimacy at its peak both Niharika And Shalini kneels down infront of Neel opening their mouths widely craving for Neels extra love....Neel shake it with full intimacy ended up by Cumming on their beautiful faces...as he feels that he were the luckiest man on earth today as he explored the beauty of his past life crush and his sweetheart Gorgeous Girlfriend together....

The unforgettable night at Neel's mansion marked a turning point in their lives. Days turned into weeks, filled with laughter, adventures, and the thrill of new experiences. Niharika and Neel shared romantic dates, while Shalini added her playful spirit to every outing. They explored new cafes, took spontaneous road trips, and enjoyed countless moments together.

As their final semester approached, the trio knew it was time to face new beginnings. After completing their exams, they gathered for one last farewell at the college, surrounded by friends, faculty, and their beloved principal. Emotions ran high as they exchanged heartfelt goodbyes, promising to stay in touch despite the paths they would soon take.

Niharika was excited yet nervous about her new job as Miss Sanjana's personal secretary at the airline. When she boarded the flight that would take her to her dream life, she felt a mix of anticipation and trepidation. After landing and settling into her chic new apartment, she pampered herself with her skincare routine before falling into a deep sleep, ready to embrace her new role.

The next morning, Niharika awoke with renewed energy, dressed impeccably in a professional attire-a tailored grey suit with a fitted blazer and a classic white blouse. The high-waisted trousers enhanced her silhouette, while her hair was styled in a sleek low bun, giving her a polished and sophisticated look. She completed the outfit with modest heels, exuding confidence as she stepped into her new office.

At the office, Miss Sanjana welcomed her with a warm smile. "I'm glad to have you on board, Niharika. Let's dive into your responsibilities."

Niharika quickly fell into her daily routine, mastering the art of organization and multitasking. Her mornings were filled with preparing agendas for meetings, taking notes, and coordinating schedules. Each day, she opted for different outfits that projected her professionalism and flair. One day, she wore a fitted emerald-green sheath dress that complemented her complexion, her hair cascading in soft waves down her shoulders. On another, she chose a classic black pencil dress, paired with a statement belt that accentuated her waist, her hair styled in a chic high ponytail.

As the days passed, Niharika became increasingly adept at handling the demands of her role. She arranged meetings, prepared presentations, and managed correspondence, showcasing her exceptional organizational skills. Her wardrobe transformed into a collection of stylish blazers, tailored trousers, and elegant blouses in varying hues-each outfit thoughtfully selected to enhance her beauty and confidence.

Occasionally, Miss Sanjana entrusted Niharika with special assignments, sending her on VIP flights as head cabin crew. Niharika relished these opportunities, donning a sleek, tailored flight attendant uniform that perfectly embodied professionalism. The uniform consisted of a fitted navy jacket with subtle silver accents, tailored trousers that flattered her figure, and a crisp white blouse. For added flair, she often wore a stylish silk scarf tied around her neck, the colors reflecting the airline's branding.

On these VIP flights, Niharika showcased her attention to detail with her immaculate grooming. She experimented with various hairstyles to match the formality of her role. One day, she styled her hair in a classic chignon, sleek and sophisticated, allowing her to move freely while maintaining an elegant appearance. On another occasion, she chose to let her hair down in soft, bouncy curls, framing her face and adding a touch of femininity to her uniform.

For particularly special flights, Niharika would opt for a polished low ponytail, accentuated with a stylish hair accessory that matched her uniform's colors, giving her a refined yet approachable look. Her makeup was always minimal yet enhancing-soft neutral tones that highlighted her features without overwhelming her natural beauty. The finishing touches included elegant stud earrings and a subtle wristwatch, exuding a refined charm.

During the flights, Niharika encountered high-profile clients, from celebrities to business moguls. She took pride in providing them with exceptional service, quickly making connections and leaving a lasting impression. During one flight, she assisted a renowned actress, who later complimented her on her professionalism and charm, inviting Niharika to stay in touch.

Another time, she served a successful entrepreneur who appreciated her attention to detail and organizational skills. Impressed by her work ethic, he offered to mentor her, opening doors to networking opportunities that Niharika eagerly accepted. These experiences not only enriched her professional life but also expanded her social circle, bringing new excitement to her career.

With each flight, Niharika returned to the office brimming with stories and insights, sharing her experiences with Miss

Sanjana, who encouraged her to aim even higher. Though the conditions of her new role remained a mystery, Niharika chose to focus on her work, determined to excel in her position.

As she settled into her new life, she looked forward to the adventures that lay ahead, embracing each moment with enthusiasm and determination. With every passing day, Niharika's journey unfolded, blending her dreams with reality and shaping her into the professional she aspired to be.

# Chapter 13

One faithful day, On a flight, Niharika sat next to Miss Sanjana, her Mentor. Miss Sanjana turned to her with a knowing smile.

• Miss Sanjana: "Do you remember what I told you on the day of your interview?"

• Niharika: "Sorry, ma'am, I forgot. Can you remind me?"

• Miss Sanjana: "Sweetheart, you're such an innocent girl. Try to remember."

• Niharika: "Is it about a meeting or work?"

• Miss Sanjana: "No, dear. You know I know your secret."

Niharika's heart raced. She suddenly recalled the day of her interview when she accidentally revealed her biggest secret.

• Niharika: "Oh no," she mumbled, her voice barely above a whisper.

• Miss Sanjana: "Thank goodness you remember. So, on that day, I mentioned you'd have to do something in exchange for keeping your secret."

• Niharika: "Yes, ma'am, you did say that."

- Miss Sanjana: "Let me ask you a few questions. Answer honestly."

- Niharika: "Of course, ma'am."

- Miss Sanjana: "Do you know Mr. John?"

- Niharika: "Sorry, ma'am, but John who?"

- Miss Sanjana: "Mr. John Mathur, of course! The richest bachelor in India?"

- Niharika: "Oh, right! Everyone knows him. He's handsome and charming."

- Miss Sanjana: "What do you and other girls think about him?"

- Niharika: "He's definitely the type every girl dreams of. He fits all the criteria."

- Miss Sanjana: "Don't you think you're one of those girls?"

- Niharika: "Um, I'm not sure what you mean, ma'am."

- Miss Sanjana: "Imagine you got a chance to go on a date with him."

Niharika felt nervous.

- Niharika: "I've never thought about it. I'm still figuring things out, but I value ambition over wealth. If he's a gentleman and kind, that's what matters to me."

- Miss Sanjana: "Perfect! That's why I like you, my dear."

- Niharika: "What do you mean, ma'am?"

- Miss Sanjana: "Let me tell you something interesting. John is my only son. He's been abroad since he was young, and no one knows I'm his mother. He's coming to India next week, and I'm introducing him as the new CEO of our airline."

• Niharika: "Wow, that's huge!"

• Miss Sanjana: "Since he needs a new secretary, I've chosen you. He's an introvert, so you'll need to interact with him and help him come out of his shell."

• Niharika: "Why me?"

• Miss Sanjana: "Because I see you as my future daughter-in-law."

Niharika's heart raced.

• Niharika: "Is this a dream?"

• Miss Sanjana: "Yes, you heard me right. You impressed me on annual day, and you have everything I want in a daughter-in-law."

• Niharika: "But ma'am, you know about my secret."

• Miss Sanjana: "I do, but I'm sure you're perfect for him. No one knows he's gay, and you're the ideal fit."

• Niharika: "What? He's gay?"

• Miss Sanjana: "Yes. I've tried everything to help him find love, but he hasn't shown interest in any girl. But I believe God sent you for a reason."

Niharika felt a mix of excitement and apprehension.

• Niharika: "I hope I can do it."

• Miss Sanjana: "You will, dear. You're amazing, and you can handle him easily."

• Niharika: "Let's see."

As the plane continued its journey, Niharika couldn't shake the mix of anticipation and nervousness about what lay ahead. Little did she know, her life was about to take an unexpected turn.

# Chapter 14

The flight landed, and as Niharika and Miss Sanjana joined their daily meeting, the routine felt familiar. After a long day, they wrapped up and headed home. That night, Niharika found herself deep in thought, wondering how she would navigate the challenges awaiting her in the morning.

Their routine included lighthearted chit-chat about work, but by the end of the evening, Miss Sanjana dropped a surprising bombshell: "Tomorrow is your holiday, but we have something important to discuss." Niharika left feeling curious and a bit anxious.

Later that night, after completing her skincare routine, she called Neel and Shalini for a conference chat. They shared stories, but Shalini had something significant to say. "Niharika, we need to tell you something important." Niharika's heart raced as Shalini revealed that she and Neel were falling for each other, reminiscing about their moments together since Niharika left university.

Niharika felt a mix of emotions; her ex-girlfriend was now with her secret boyfriend. She ended the call with tears of joy and sadness, unsure of how to feel. Sleep was elusive as thoughts swirled in her mind about what the next day would bring.

Morning arrived, her holiday finally here. Niharika chose a stunning outfit: a light, flowing sundress that hugged her figure perfectly, paired with strappy sandals. She styled her hair in a sleek ponytail secured with a vibrant scrunchie, which highlighted her features and gave her a playful yet chic look. With a touch of makeup that accentuated her natural beauty, she felt radiant and confident as she left her apartment.

As she called Miss Sanjana, she received a location. When Niharika arrived, she was greeted by a lavish café where Miss Sanjana was waiting.

Sipping their coffees, Miss Sanjana said, "It's your responsibility now to make John fall for you." She shared details about John, painting a picture of the perfect man. "He's not just good-looking; he's incredibly passionate about photography and often spends weekends capturing the beauty of nature. He also plays the guitar beautifully and loves to cook traditional dishes. You should hear him talk about his favorite recipes!"

Niharika felt her heart race. "He sounds amazing!"

"Absolutely! And he's an avid traveler, always exploring new places and cultures. He even writes a travel blog, sharing his adventures and the dishes he learns to make from different countries," Miss Sanjana continued, her eyes sparkling with excitement.

"Wow, I can't believe I've never noticed how perfect he is!" Niharika said, feeling both thrilled and nervous.

"Time for some shopping for my dear sweetheart!" Miss Sanjana declared, her eyes twinkling with mischief. As they strolled through the mall, they visited several stores, trying on stylish outfits and giggling at each other's choices.

"Try this one!" Miss Sanjana insisted, handing Niharika a beautiful saree that accentuated her curves. "John will be mesmerized!" They spent time in a cute accessory shop, where Miss Sanjana playfully insisted Niharika try on some bold earrings, exclaiming, "These will make you look irresistible!"

Then came the fun part: lingerie shopping. Miss Sanjana teased, "You never know when you might need something special for that special day!" Niharika blushed but couldn't help but laugh at Miss Sanjana's playful nudging. They shared jokes and laughter as they browsed, creating a carefree atmosphere.

After their shopping spree, Miss Sanjana revealed she had made an appointment for both of them at a special parlor the next day. Niharika felt thrilled; it was a delightful surprise at every turn.

Returning home, she felt a newfound happiness for Shalini and Neel, but her mind buzzed with curiosity about her own new chapter. She opened Instagram and searched for

John's profile. When she found it, her eyes widened. He was strikingly handsome with a fit physique—nothing like she had imagined.

Scrolling through his pictures, her heart raced at a shirtless photo that revealed his muscular build. Each image drew her closer to the thought of him. That night, she found herself daydreaming about the charming moments they could share. As she lay in bed, she let her imagination run wild, picturing sweet and tender scenarios with John that made her smile.

With every thought of him, excitement bubbled within her, and she couldn't help but feel a thrill at the possibilities ahead. The night wrapped around her like a warm blanket as she drifted off to sleep, her dreams filled with visions of John, making her heart flutter with anticipation.

# Chapter 15

Niharika stood at the entrance of the lavish ballroom, her elegant attire flowing gracefully around her. She wore a stunning emerald green gown that hugged her curves, the fabric shimmering under the soft lights. Her hair was styled in loose, cascading waves, adorned with delicate pins that twinkled like stars. As she gazed toward the entrance, a blur of a handsome man approached, the clarity sharpening as he drew near.

Her heart raced, and her breath caught in her throat. He reached her, placing a warm hand on her waist, pulling her close. Their eyes locked, and he leaned in, planting a gentle, genuine kiss on her soft lips. She savored the taste of his lip gloss, her mind lost in the moment.

Suddenly, the blaring sound of her alarm shattered the dream. Niharika mumbled, "It's just a dream," a playful smile gracing her lips as she remembered the appointment awaiting her today with Miss Sanjana. She quickly opened her gallery, kissing the screen of a shirtless photo of Mr. John, murmuring, "Morning, handsome."

After a quick shower and minimal makeup, she chose a chic yet comfortable outfit—a fitted white blouse paired with high-waisted jeans and elegant heels. Checking her phone, she saw a message from Miss Sanjana with the location of the parlor.

Upon arriving, she found Miss Sanjana waiting, arms crossed and a teasing smile on her face. "Where have you been, sweetie? We're late! You should be punctual; your future boyfriend is very punctual," she joked, both women laughing as they exchanged knowing glances.

As they stepped inside, Niharika was mesmerized by the parlor's opulence. The space exuded luxury: chandeliers sparkled overhead, plush velvet chairs lined the walls, and the air was infused with the scent of exotic perfumes. Mirrors framed in gold reflected the serene ambiance, while beautiful floral arrangements adorned every corner. It was a beauty haven she had only dreamed of.

"Is this place for real?" Niharika exclaimed, her eyes wide with awe.

"Of course, sweetie! You're going to meet the most handsome bachelor, so you need to be perfect," Miss Sanjana replied. "Remember, first impressions last."

They were soon greeted by the owner, a stylish woman who treated them like special guests. "Let's get started!" she announced with a warm smile.

The pampering began with a soothing skincare regimen that left Niharika's skin glowing. They applied rejuvenating masks and serums, followed by a gentle facial massage that made her feel like royalty.

Next, her hair was expertly styled; they added soft curls and a touch of sparkle with elegant hair accessories.

Afterward, Niharika was guided to the nail station, where her nails were meticulously manicured and painted a soft blush pink, complementing her attire perfectly. As she admired her hands, she felt more confident than ever.

Finally, they moved to the makeup station, where a talented artist enhanced her features with a natural yet glamorous look. Niharika glanced in the mirror, barely recognizing the stunning woman staring back at her.

Just as they wrapped up, Miss Sanjana whispered, "Are you ready for tomorrow? I have a feeling it's going to be unforgettable."

As Niharika exited the parlor, her heart raced with excitement and nerves. She couldn't shake the feeling that something extraordinary awaited her. But just then, her phone buzzed with a new message. Curious, she glanced at the screen—it was a video call request from Neel, her ex-boyfriend and good friend.

Hesitating for a moment, she answered. The screen lit up to reveal Neel, looking as charming as ever. "Wow, Niharika! You look absolutely stunning!" he exclaimed, his eyes wide with admiration. "Is this for someone special or new one, huh ?"

"Thanks, Neel! It is. I can't believe tomorrow is finally happening," she replied, a mix of excitement and nervousness bubbling inside her.

"I had to call you. I wanted to make sure you know how incredible you look. And honestly, you deserve to be treated like a queen," he said, a hint of sincerity in his voice.

Niharika felt a warmth spread in her chest. "That means a lot, especially coming from you."

"Listen, if he doesn't sweep you off your feet, you know I'm just a call away," Neel teased, his playful grin brightening the screen.

"Don't you have a your new girlfriend now?" she quipped back, knowing he was dating shalini.

"Yeah, but she doesn't have to know about our little code, right?" he winked, and they both laughed. But as their conversation continued, Niharika couldn't shake the feeling that Neel's eyes held something more than just friendship.

As they ended the call, she couldn't help but wonder: did Neel still have feelings for her? And what would tomorrow hold? With questions swirling in her mind, she took a deep breath, realizing that not only was she about to meet Mr. John, but the unresolved tension with Neel lingered, adding an unexpected layer of complexity to her day. Tomorrow was bound to be even more intriguing than she had imagined.

# Chapter 16

Niharika tossed and turned in her sleep, her mind filled with a mix of emotions. In her dream, she was on a perfect date with Neel, laughter and warmth enveloping them and they ended up making out with eachother.

But as the morning sun broke through her curtains, reality set in. She woke up feeling confused, whispering to herself, "Why do I still dream about him? It's over now. I have a new chapter ahead."

Determined to embrace her fresh start, she began her skincare routine, carefully cleansing and moisturizing her face. Today, she decided to indulge in a special bath. She filled the tub with warm water and added fragrant essential oils-lavender for relaxation and chamomile for clarity. The steam enveloped her, soothing her mind and body, preparing her for the day ahead.

After her bath, Niharika dressed with intention. She selected a sophisticated navy blazer over a cream silk blouse, paired with tailored charcoal trousers that accentuated her figure while exuding professionalism. A pair of sleek, pointed-toe heels completed the look, making her feel empowered. She tied her hair back with a soft pink ribbon, allowing a few loose strands to frame her face elegantly.

Leaving her apartment, she met Miss Sanjana, who beamed at her. "You look stunning, Niharika! Just perfect for John's arrival," she said, handing over the final instructions for the day. Niharika felt a flutter of excitement as she absorbed the details about John's arrival and the arrangements in place.

Taking charge, she headed to the airport in a sleek convoy. As she arrived, Niharika was taken aback by the crowd waiting for John.

Instead of the usual sea of male fans, there were groups of young women, all eagerly anticipating his arrival. "It's alright, Niharika; you're the boss," she murmured, standing confidently at the arrival gate, holding a beautiful bouquet of flowers with a welcome note attached.

As the doors opened, John made a grand entrance, striding toward her with undeniable charisma. He was strikingly handsome, his presence commanding attention. Her heart raced as he approached, and to her astonishment, he pulled her close and kissed her cheek. The sound of applause jolted her back to reality, and she blinked, trying to process the moment.

"Thanks for the warm welcome, Niharika," he said, leaning in to take the bouquet from her hands. "I assume this is for me?"

"Oh, yes! Mr. John, welcome to India!" she replied, her cheeks flushing.

John smiled and asked about the convoy, and as they walked to the car, Niharika reminded herself, "It was just a dream. Wake up, Niharika." They engaged in light chitchat during the drive, easing her nerves.

Upon reaching the office, Miss Sanjana warmly welcomed her son and introduced him to the team. As they settled into the cabin, she emphasized Niharika's role as John's new secretary, urging him to share any requests with her.

Soon, Miss Sanjana announced a grand party to celebrate John's new position as CEO, inviting VIP guests, celebrities, and media. Niharika felt the weight of responsibility as Miss Sanjana insisted she look perfect for the event.

For the party, Niharika chose a stunning deep red gown that hugged her curves elegantly, complemented by subtle gold accessories. She styled her hair in an intricate updo, securing it with the elegant ribbon, which added a touch of charm to her sophisticated look. As the event kicked off, John captivated the crowd from his main chair, radiating charm and confidence.

Niharika expertly led the proceedings, but as she stepped forward to present John with flowers as a gesture of appreciation, disaster struck-her sandal broke, and she slipped. In a split second, John caught her, and their eyes locked in a moment that felt almost romantic, like a scene from a movie.

Miss Sanjana beamed at the sight, and the media quickly captured the moment.

"Sorry about that," Niharika stammered, flustered.

"Maybe you should say thanks instead, silly girl," John replied with a teasing smile.

"Oh, right! Thank you, Mr. John," she managed to say, feeling both embarrassed and thrilled. The party continued with laughter and chatter, gossip buzzing among guests about the new CEO and his charming assistant.

As the night wound down, Miss Sanjana thanked everyone for attending, reminding Niharika to be on time the next day. "It's your first day with our new CEO!"

"Yes, boss!" Niharika exclaimed, leaving the venue with a mix of excitement and nervousness.

Back in her room, her mind replayed the evening's events, especially the moment with John. She felt a blend of exhilaration and anxiety about what lay ahead. Thoughts of their shared laughter and the electric connection filled her mind as she prepared for bed, her heart racing at the possibilities of tomorrow. With a smile on her face, she finally drifted into sleep, dreaming not just of her past, but of a promising future.

# Chapter 17

The next morning, Niharika got ready and arrived at the office sharp at 8 AM, knowing Mr. John was always punctual. When he walked in, he smiled and said, "I appreciate you being on time. I like punctual people."

Niharika beamed at his compliment and eagerly asked about their work. "Chill, Miss Secretary," he replied playfully. "Let me take care of our office. No need to be a bullet train!"

They shared a few laughs and exchanged light-hearted banter, enjoying the budding camaraderie. As the day wrapped up, Niharika prepared to leave, turning to John and saying, "Goodbye, Mr. John!"

"From now on, just call me John," he said, raising an eyebrow.

With a confused look, Niharika replied, "Okay, Mr. John..."

John chuckled, "Ahh, sorry, just John!"

"Oh, ugh, John, John," she mumbled to herself, flustered. With a nervous smile, she waved goodbye and left, while John shook his head, muttering, "Silly girl," a grin spreading across his face.

Later that night, Niharika received a call from Neel. They enjoyed some light chit-chat, and Shalini soon joined the conversation, filling the air with gossip. After hanging up, her phone buzzed again. It was John.

Her heart raced as she answered, "Hi, Miss Secretary!" he teased.

"Yes, sir. What do you want?" Niharika replied, trying to maintain her composure.

"Is it that I have to call you only for work?" he asked, the playful tone evident.

"Um, absolutely not, sir. I'm sorry..." she stammered.

"Don't be sorry," he teased, his voice warm.

Niharika giggled, feeling her nerves settle. "Okay, what's up?"

"Let me get to the point," John said, his tone shifting slightly. "Tomorrow, we have an important meeting. Be ready in your cabin crew uniform; we're meeting someone special."

Curiosity piqued, Niharika asked, "Are they from our industry, sir?"

"Nope, Miss Secretary. She's more than that," he replied, a hint of mystery in his voice.

"Who is she?" Niharika thought, her mind racing. "Is she more beautiful than me? Is she his girlfriend? But wait, isn't John gay?"

She shook her head, trying to dismiss the whirlwind of thoughts. "Ahh, Niharika, stop thinking!" she chided herself as she settled into bed, sleep creeping in.

The next morning, Niharika was determined to look more stunning than the girl John had mentioned. She chose a form-fitting cabin crew uniform that accentuated her figure and expertly styled her hair into a sleek braid adorned with colorful ribbons. She felt confident and beautiful as she prepared for the day.

Excitedly, she called John, but he cut the call, texting her the location instead. Her heart raced as she read the message, and with butterflies in her stomach, she left her apartment.

Arriving at the location, Niharikagasped as she spotted a private jet on the long runway. Curiosity sparked within her. She called John, and he picked up, instructing her to come to the flight. As she approached, a staff member opened the door and asked for her car keys. Niharika handed them over, her heart pounding as she joined John on the private jet.

When she saw him, her heartbeats quickened. Was this what love felt like? She brushed the thought aside, trying to focus on the moment. John gestured for her to take a seat, and as he waved his hand, the pilot began the takeoff.

"Nervous?" John asked, glancing over at her.

"Where are we going?" she asked, her excitement mingled with anxiety.

"Just be quiet and enjoy the ride," he teased, leaving her in suspense.

Once they landed, Niharika's eyes widened as she saw the most luxurious car she had always dreamed about. John opened the door for her and urged her to get in. As he drove, he asked, "So, tell me about yourself, silly girl."

Wanting to keep her true identity a secret, she concocted an imaginary story about her life, and they chatted comfortably. Their laughter filled the car, and Niharika felt a bond growing stronger with every passing moment.

As they arrived at their destination, Niharika realized they were at an aquarium restaurant beneath the sea. "Wow, this is incredible!" she exclaimed, her eyes sparkling with wonder.

They sat at a beautifully set table, surrounded by the mesmerizing view of colorful fish swimming by. "So, where's the girl you were talking about yesterday?" she asked, a hint of curiosity in her voice.

With a mischievous smile, John replied, "She'll meet you soon."

He ordered an array of delicious dishes, and Niharika hesitated to eat. "I don't want to impose," she said, feeling slightly out of her league.

John reassured her, "You're not imposing; just enjoy!" As she took a bite, her eyes widened in delight. "Wow, this is amazing!"

"Yep, it's my favorite," he said, grinning.

They continued to chat and laugh, their connection deepening with each passing moment. After finishing their meal, John suggested they leave, and soon they arrived at the most luxurious hotel in town.

"Is the girl here?" Niharika asked, hoping for some clarity.

John playfully ignored her question, saying, "You'll meet her soon." Frustrated yet intrigued, she followed him inside, where he checked them into two separate rooms.

"You'll meet her tomorrow at our office party," John said casually.

"Office party? I didn't know about this!" Niharika exclaimed, her surprise evident.

"Oh, you silly girl! You've been with me all day; how could you miss that I announced it?" he teased.

Niharika sighed, "Okay, sorry. I guess I got caught up in everything."

John added, "We need to leave for the party location tomorrow morning, so be ready on time." With that, he walked into his room, leaving Niharika with a mix of emotions swirling inside her. She lay in bed, excitement and anxiety battling for dominance, and eventually drifted off to sleep, dreaming of what tomorrow would bring.

# Chapter 18

The soft sunlight streamed through the hotel window, gently kissing Niharika's face and pulling her from sleep. As she began her morning skincare routine, the doorbell rang.

She opened the door to find a hotel staff member holding a large, beautifully wrapped gift box adorned with a satin ribbon.

"This is from Mr. John," he said with a polite smile.

"Where's John?" Niharika asked, her curiosity piqued.

"They've already checked out," he replied, leaving her momentarily stunned. "What the...?" she exclaimed, her mind racing as she rook the box.

With eager anticipation, she carefully opened it, gasping at the sight within. Inside lay a stunning, intricately designed saree in a rich royal blue, adorned with delicate silver embroidery that shimmered under the light. The saree draped elegantly, accentuating her hourglass figure, and the fabric cascaded like water, exuding both grace and sophistication.

Accompanying the saree were exquisite jewelry boxes filled with pie pri jces that sparkled with diamonds and sapphires, crafted to perfection. There was a statement necklace that rested delicately against her collarbone, with matching earrings that caught the light with every movement. Each item seemed to whisper luxury and sophistication.

Nestled among the treasures was a heartfelt note. Unfolding it, she felt her heart race as she began to read:

"Hey, silly girl, it's John here! This is for you because I want you to look your best for the party. I'm introducing someone special to you, so get ready to shine!"

There was also a note about a car pickup for her. Anger bubbled within her. "What the heck is he thinking? He wants to introduce me to his girlfriend?" she thought, her mind swirling with questions. Determined to show him that no one could outshine her, she decided to reveal her most stunning self.

Niharika spent hours getting ready, selecting the perfect makeup that highlighted her features. She chose to wear her long, jet-black hair in an elegant braided updo, with soft, cascading curls framing her face. Delicate ribbons, in hues that mirrored the saree's color, adorned her hair, adding a touch of whimsy and sophistication. When she was finally satisfied with her look, she stepped back to admire herself in the mirror—a vision of timeless beauty.

Once ready, she made her way to the front desk, where the staff informed her, "The bill is already settled, ma'am. The car is waiting for you outside."

As she stepped into the waiting luxury car, her heart raced with excitement. The vehicle glided to a stunning resort, a place filled with vibrant colors and elegant decor, buzzing with anticipation. Celebrities and media were already gathered outside, the atmosphere alive with flashes of cameras and murmurs of admiration.

Upon entering, Niharika was greeted by Miss Sanjana. "Oh my, look who's here! You're absolutely killing it with your look, my sweetie!" Sanjana exclaimed, her eyes wide with admiration. "But why this sudden glamour?"

"It's John's idea," Niharika replied, her tone a mix of pride and confusion.

With curiosity dancing in her eyes, Sanjana asked, "Is it true, Niharika?"

"Yes, ma'am," Niharika confirmed, feeling a rush of excitement as they joined the festivities. The energy in the room was electric, filled with laughter and animated conversations.

As the party commenced, the sounds of joy echoed throughout the resort. Suddenly, a glass clinked against a spoon, capturing everyone's attention. It was John, holding a microphone, ready to address the crowd.

"Today is my best day, and you'll soon understand why!" he announced, his voice resonating through the room. Niharika shot him a mock glare, anticipating his introduction of her to his girlfriend.

"Before that, I'd like to invite Niharika and my mom, Miss Sanjana, onto the stage," he called out.

They walked up, the spotlight illuminating them. John began to speak, sharing his journey of achievements and struggles. As he spoke, his voice grew softer, revealing a vulnerable side that made Niharika's heart race.

"I have everything I could ever want, except true friendship," he continued. "I've always been alone and never really interested in any girl. But after meeting Niharika, I started to feel happy. I wanted her around me."

Sanjana's eyes sparkled with excitement, seeing her son in such a new light. Niharika, however, felt a mix of emotions—confusion and anger intertwined as she tried to process his words.

Then, John revealed the truth. "She is none other than Miss Niharika!" The room fell silent, everyone stunned. Niharika felt a wave of disbelief wash over her, and Sanjana gently nudged her to regain her senses.

Taking a step forward, Niharika's heart swelled with emotions she never expected. John knelt down, looking deeply into her eyes. "You've been asking me since yesterday who she is. Now look into my eyes and see for yourself."

As she gazed into his warm, expressive eyes, Niharika saw not just his reflection but her own happiness mirrored back. John opened a ring box, revealing a beautiful ring. "Will you be mine forever?"

Tears of joy streamed down her face as she extended her hand. "Yes!" she whispered, shaking her head in disbelief. John slid the ring onto her finger, and the room erupted in cheers and applause, celebrating their love.

As the news spread through the town, Sanjana enveloped Niharika in a warm hug. "You did it, sweetie!" she said, her voice filled with pride.

"Yes, Mom!" Niharika replied, her heart overflowing with happiness. The night was just beginning, and she knew this was only the start of an extraordinary journey ahead, with the world watching and celebrating their love.

# Chapter 19

● The Morning After: A New Chapter for Niharika :

The sun had barely risen when the town of Mathur erupted into celebration. It was now official-Niharika was declared the future daughter-in-law of the prestigious Mathur family. Billboards across the city displayed the smiling faces of Niharika and John, the picture-perfect couple, while news channels buzzed with excitement. Every news outlet featured stories about their upcoming wedding, labeling it the event of the year. Wherever Niharika went, the media followed, capturing every smile, every wave. She had transformed into a celebrity overnight, and she was enjoying every moment of her newfound fame.

The people in town couldn't stop talking about the wedding. It wasn't just going to be big; it was going to be grand.

A wedding of the century. And everyone wanted to be part of it. Niharika was flooded with congratulations from friends, acquaintances, and even strangers who now knew her as "the future Mathur bride."

One evening, as Niharika was winding down after yet another day of media frenzy, her phone rang. She glanced at the screen and smiled-Shalini. Her heart warmed at the sight of her best friend's name. It had been so long since they'd spoken, and Shalini, once her girlfriend and still her closest confidante, had been absent from her life for far too long.

Niharika answered the call, her voice bubbling with excitement. "Shalini! Oh my God, it's been forever!"

Shalini's voice, equally joyful, rang through the phone. "I know! You're famous now! Every time I turn on the TV, there's Niharika, the star! How does it feel?"

Niharika laughed, the sound filled with both joy and a bit of disbelief. "It's surreal! Everywhere I go, the cameras follow. But honestly, it's a lot of fun. You know how much I love the spotlight."

Shalini chuckled. "Oh, I remember. Always the drama queen."

Niharika's tone softened. "Hey, I want you to be part of all this, Shalini. I'm getting married in a month, and I need you here. You've got to be one of my bridesmaids."

There was a brief pause on the other end, followed by a soft laugh. "You think I'd miss it? Of course, I'll be there."

They shared a few more laughs, catching up on old times, reminiscing about their past before the conversation moved to the future. As Niharika hung up, she felt a sense of completeness. Her life was evolving, and she was glad to have Shalini by her side for this next chapter.

• Preparations Begin: Miss Sanjana's Perfectionism :

As the wedding date loomed closer, the Mathur family, led by John's mother, Miss Sanjana, kicked the wedding preparations into high gear. Miss Sanjana was determined to make Niharika the most perfect bride anyone had ever seen. She wasn't just overseeing the wedding arrangements-she had an army of professionals to ensure her future daughter-in-law was flawless for the big day.

Miss Sanjana had spared no expense. She hired a personal trainer, a diet specialist, and even a stylist to craft Niharika's look for the wedding. "Niharika, darling," she said one afternoon while overseeing one of the sessions. "We need to make sure you're in the best shape of your life. A Mathur bride must be perfect-inside and out."

Niharika, always eager to please but slightly overwhelmed, smiled. "Of course, Miss Sanjana."

• Girly Days with Miss Sanjana :

But it wasn't all pressure. Miss Sanjana had a softer side, especially when it came to spending time with Niharika. They'd spend mornings together visiting exclusive boutiques, looking at fabrics, jewelry, and shoes. Miss Sanjana loved to discuss bridal fashion trends and critique every outfit they saw.

"Niharika, sweetheart," Miss Sanjana said one afternoon while they were sipping tea at an upscale boutique. "The lehenga for the wedding should shimmer like stars but still maintain elegance. We'll get you a custom-made one that complements your skin tone."

Niharika, sipping her tea, admired the swatches of fabric in front of them. "I trust your judgment, Miss Sanjana. You have an eye for these things."

Miss Sanjana beamed, clearly pleased. They spent hours flipping through bridal catalogs and picking out Niharika's outfits for the endless pre-wedding events. The two of them had become close during these outings, with Miss Sanjana treating her more like a daughter than just the future bride of her son.

• Workouts and the Perfect Silhouette :

Of course, there was still the matter of getting Niharika into the perfect shape for her wedding day. Her diet specialist put her on a carefully planned meal regimen, ensuring that every calorie was accounted for. Meals became a balance between indulgence and discipline, with beautifully plated but light dishes.

Her personal trainer was a no-nonsense woman who ensured Niharika was toned but not too muscular, aiming for that perfect bridal silhouette. Every morning began with a grueling yoga session followed by a mix of Pilates and weight training.

"You're doing great, Niharika," the trainer encouraged as Niharika worked through another set of core exercises. "We'll have you in that lehenga and looking like a goddess in no time."

John often couldn't resist popping into her workout sessions, his grin teasing as always. "You're working too hard," he said one morning as she was mid-pose in a yoga session. He leaned casually against the doorframe, arms crossed. "You're already stunning. Are they trying to turn you into some kind of superhero?"

Niharika shot him a playful glare. "If I have to do one more plank, I might actually turn into one."

John chuckled and walked over, dropping a kiss on her forehead. "You've always been my hero, anyway."

Niharika smiled, a mix of exhaustion and happiness. "You'd better keep up that charm when I'm walking down the aisle."

"Oh, I plan on it," he whispered, before leaving her to her workout, the image of his playful grin stuck in her mind.

• Miss Sanjana's Watchful Eye :

As the wedding drew nearer, the fittings for Niharika's bridal attire became more frequent. One afternoon, she stood in front of a mirror in an elegant bridal gown, her silhouette already looking flawless after weeks of training and diet. The gown, with its intricate embroidery and delicate veil, made her feel like she was truly living a fairy tale.

Miss Sanjana circled her, inspecting every inch. "Hmm...the waist could be more defined. And the neckline-make sure it complements the jewelry. We can't have anything overshadowing the diamonds."

Niharika stifled a laugh. "Miss Sanjana, are the diamonds really the main attraction?"

Miss Sanjana raised an eyebrow, though her smile betrayed her amusement. "In a Mathur wedding, everything is the main attraction, dear."

The fittings were long, but Niharika couldn't deny the excitement building within her. She was being transformed into the perfect bride, and though the process was rigorous, there was a thrill in watching herself evolve.

• Celebration Buzz: The Grand Wedding Announcement :

Then came the grand announcement. One fine day, Miss Sanjana declared the official wedding date of John and Niharika. The news spread like wildfire-social media, news outlets, billboards-all buzzing with the excitement of the upcoming wedding. "The grandest wedding Mathur town has ever seen!" was the headline on every network.

The celebrations began long before the actual wedding, with parties, events, and even special features about Niharika and John's love story running on news channels. Invitations were sent out to the who's who of society, and the guest list seemed endless.

One evening, as Niharika tried on yet another outfit for an upcoming pre-wedding party, John appeared at the door, his familiar teasing grin in place. "Another fitting? At this rate, we might need an entire closet just for your wedding outfits."

Niharika turned, a smile playing on her lips. "Well, someone has to keep up with all the expectations around here."

He stepped closer, brushing a loose strand of hair from her face. "You'll be more than enough, Niharika. You always are."

She smiled, warmth filling her heart. "And you'll still be there waiting for me at the altar, right?"

John's eyes sparkled as he whispered, "Always."

• A Month to Go: Perfection in the Making :

With only a month left before the wedding, everything was moving quickly. Miss Sanjana's team of professionals continued to shape Niharika into the "perfect" bride. The diet specialist monitored her meals meticulously, the trainers kept her active, and the stylists worked on perfecting her look for the big day.

Amidst all the chaos, Niharika found joy in the small moments-John's teasing, her phone calls with Shalini, and the support of her soon-to-be family. The anticipation was building, and with every passing day, Niharika felt herself growing more confident and ready for the spotlight. She had stepped into her role as the future Mathur bride, and there was no turning back.

The grandest wedding the town had ever seen was on the horizon, and Niharika was ready to embrace her new life, not just as John's bride, but as a Mathur.....

# Chapter 20

A Week to Go: The Grand Wedding Looms :

With just a week left until the wedding, Mathur town was abuzz with excitement. Every street was adorned with lights, and billboards of Niharika and John announced the wedding of the century. The media was relentless, following Niharika everywhere, and she basked in the spotlight.

The grand preparations were complete. Lavish decorations filled the venues, and high-profile guests were flying in. Every corner of her life now revolved around the big day, and with every passing hour, her excitement grew.

• Shalini's Arrival and Neel's Surprising Appearance :

When Shalini finally arrived, Niharika was overjoyed, but she was surprised to find Neel-her past boyfriend-at her side. Laughing, she hugged them both.

"Well, this is a twist!" Niharika exclaimed.

Neel smirked, eyes glinting with mischief. "Couldn't resist crashing the grand wedding prep."

As they caught up, Neel couldn't help but notice Niharika's transformation. "You look... different, Niharika. Stunning, really. Must be all that bride-to-be magic."

Niharika laughed, brushing off the compliment. "I guess the bridal workouts are paying off."

But Neel didn't let it go, his eyes teasing. "It's more than that. You've got that whole 'perfect bride' silhouette now. It's turning heads, for sure."

Shalini rolled her eyes, nudging Neel playfully. "Alright, enough. She's already taken."

• Pre-Wedding Rituals: Niharika's Stunning Looks :

With the wedding week packed full of pre-wedding rituals and parties, Niharika's wardrobe and beauty were the talk of the town.

At the mehendi ceremony, she dazzled in a vibrant emerald-green lehenga, her long, glossy hair adorned with jasmine flowers, styled in a soft, romantic braid. Her delicate hands were covered in intricate henna designs, and the guests couldn't stop admiring her elegance.

For the sangeet, Niharika stunned everyone in a deep red and gold saree, paired with a bold smokey-eye look. Her hair was swept into an elegant bun, accentuated with gold pins. The event was lively, with music and dancing, and John couldn't take his eyes off her.

"She's a vision," Neel whispered to Shalini as he watched Niharika twirl on the dance floor, clearly mesmerized by her.

• Final Shopping Spree with Miss Sanjana :

Miss Sanjana, ever the perfectionist, took Niharika and Shalini on one final shopping trip to ensure everything was flawless. At the boutique, Niharika tried on exquisite sarees and lehengas, each one more stunning than the last. A royal blue lehenga for the cocktail party, paired with a sleek ponytail, was Miss Sanjana's favorite.

"You're going to outshine every star in the sky," Miss Sanjana declared, inspecting the intricate beadwork.

Even Neel couldn't resist teasing. "Better keep some of the shine for the actual wedding day, Niharika."

• Neel's Teasing and a Glimpse of thCountdown :

As the preparations intensified, Niharika spent more time with Shalini and Neel, recalling old memories. One evening, as they relaxed in the garden, Neel teased her again. "Remember when you swore you'd have a tiny, intimate wedding? Now look at you-Miss Mathur, starring in the wedding of the decade."

Niharika laughed, shaking her head. "Life changes, Neel. And honestly, I'm loving every minute of it."

Neel leaned in, his voice softer, "You've changed too. That confidence, the way you carry yourself now... it's something else."

For a brief moment, Niharika felt the weight of his words, but she quickly shook it off. "Maybe it's the bridal glow," she joked.

But Neel's gaze lingered, a teasing smile playing on his lips. "Or maybe it's just you."

The Final Countdown…

As the week flew by, Niharika embraced each day with excitement. She balanced pre-wedding rituals with the joy of spending time with her closest friends, and even Neel's playful teasing added warmth to the chaos.

Every day, she dazzled in stunning outfits, from pastel sarees to embellished gowns, with hairstyles that accentuated her new, confident beauty. The countdown to the wedding had begun, and Niharika felt more ready than ever to step into her new life as a Miss Mathur.

# Chapter 21

Before wedding day...

Niharika: Still in her room, trying on her wedding lingerie and putting on a garter belt, she suddenly hears the door close behind her. She turns to see Neel standing there with a sly grin. Neel.. what are you doing here? Though slightly surprised, she can't help but feel a dash of excitement at his appearance - he was always good at catching her off guard.

Neel: He walks closer, his eyes roaming over Niharika's body appreciatively as she turns side to side, admiring her reflection. I couldn't resist seeing my girl one last time before the big day. And I must say... His gaze lingers on the delicate lace of her lingerie. You look incredible. Like every man's dream.

He steps behind her, resting his hands on her hips as he peers over her shoulder at her reflection. I've always wanted one last night with you before you become Mrs. Mathur. A night to remember... His voice is low and husky with desire.

Niharika: She bites her lip, feeling a rush of arousal at his words. She knew this might happen someday, but never thought it would be before the wedding night. Neel... we shouldn't...it's so close to the big day...

Neel: Then it's now or never, sweetheart. His hand slides up to caress the small of her back as he presses against her from behind. You're perfect, Niharika. I wonder how many times John will make you scream like this.

With a sudden movement, he spins Niharika around to face him and crashes his lips against hers in a heated kiss.

Niharika: She gasps into the passionate kiss, wrapping her arms around Neel's neck as she melts into him. Her lips part eagerly, and she kisses him back with equal fervor, years of suppressed desire bursting forth.

Neel: His hands roam greedily over her body, tracing the curves of her breasts through the sheer fabric before sliding down to grip her hips. I'm going to make you feel so good, baby. One last time...

He pushes her back onto the bed, his kisses becoming more desperate as he rips open her silk robe, exposing her naked body to his hungry eyes. He drinks in every inch of her curves and marks on her skin.

Niharika: She arches beneath him, moaning shamelessly at his mere touch. The wedding nerves have transformed into pure lust. Neel, fuck me...please...

He smirks at her wanton demand and trails a hand down to tease her damp folds, groaning at how wet she already is. I'll give you everything you've been craving, my love.

As he exploring her....

Neel: He smirks, surprise flickering across his features as he realizes what he's seeing. What the hell is this?

Neel gazes at Niharika's artificial pussy with a mix of surprise and arousal. "A pussy?

When did you get this made?" He asks, his eyes gleaming with intrigue as his fingers trace the smooth, slick folds. "Niharika: She blushes, averting her gaze. "I got it made for my wedding night, Neel. As a little surprise. It's artificial but works just as well as the real thing..." She winks teasingly, biting her lower lip.

Neel smirks, desire burning in his eyes as he leans in to run his tongue along the length of her new slit. "Mmmm, you naughty girl... hiding this secret from me. Lucky I found it before your wedding night..."

He murmurs huskily between licks, probing her tight hole with the tip of his tongue.

Niharika lets out a gasp, her back arching

Niharika lets out a shuddering moan as Neel's tongue delves deeper into her artificial pussy, stroking along the slick walls. Ohhh Neel, yesss... she hisses, threading her fingers through his hair to pull him closer.

He grins against her folds, the vibrations adding to her pleasure. Mmmm, you taste divine, baby. I could eat this sweet cunt for hours... His words are muffled but dripping with lust as he laps hungrily at her, swirling his tongue around her clit.

Niharika writhes beneath him, her thighs clamping around his head as her climax builds. Neel, I'm...I'm gonna cum! she cries out, her voice high and breathless with need.

Neel doubles his efforts, sucking and licking Niharika's clit as he plunges two fingers knuckle-deep into her dripping hole, stroking along her walls. That's it, baby, cum for me... he growls, his voice vibrating against her sensitive flesh.

Niharika screams out her pleasure, her body shaking violently as an intense orgasm crashes through her. Her pussy spasms around Neel's fingers, gushing with juices. OHHH FUCK YES! I'M CUMMING! she wails, her nails digging into his scalp.

Neel laps up her release greedily, prolonging her climax with expert strokes and sucks until she's boneless and panting, her legs trembling. Mmmm, you cum so sweet, Niharika... he purrs, crawling up her body to capture her lips in a passionate kiss, letting her taste herself on his tongue.

Neel pulls back from the kiss, his eyes dark with lust as he gazes down at Niharika's flushed, satisfied face. I can't believe you hid this sexy surprise from me... He murmurs, trailing a finger along the slick folds of her artificial pussy. But I'm glad

I found it before your wedding night. Now I get to be the first to break in this tight little cunt.

Niharika blushes, biting her lower lip coyly. I wanted it to be special for John...but I guess you'll just have to seal it up again with your cum. She reaches down to stroke his hard, throbbing cock teasingly. Think you can handle that, big boy?

Neel groans, thrusting into her hand. Oh, I'll more than handle it, baby. I'm going to fuck this pussy so good, you'll forget all about your wedding night plans...

Niharika bites her lip, her eyes gleaming with mischief as she traces the outline of Neel's hard cock through his pants. Mmmm, I'm counting on it, stud. But can you really satisfy me better than John? I've heard he's quite the lover... She teases, squeezing his shaft and reveling in his groan.

Neel's jaw clenches, a possessive glint in his eye as he grips Niharika's hips tighter. Trust me, baby, I'll ruin you for anyone else. By the time I'm done with this pussy, you won't even remember John's name. In a swift move, he flips Niharika onto her stomach, pulling her hips up so she's on all fours, her ass in the air. He kneels behind her, giving her ass a firm slap that makes her yelp and moan. Neel, yes! Mark me!

# Chapter 22

Neel smirks as he kneels behind Niharika's upturned ass, giving her firm cheeks a hard spank. The sharp crack of skin on skin echoes through the room, followed by Niharika's pleasured yelp.

"Mmm, you like that, don't you slut?" He growls, rubbing the reddened flesh before delivering another stinging slap to the other cheek. "Such a naughty bride, getting spanked by her ex the night before her wedding..."

Niharika moans shamelessly, arching her back to present herself fully to Neel. "Yes, Neel! Fuck, I've missed your hands on me..." She reaches back to spread her ass, exposing her dripping artificial pussy to his hungry gaze.

Neel licks his lips, taking in the sight of her slick folds, glistening with arousal. "Fuck, you're so wet for me already..." He positions himself at her entrance, rubbing the swollen head of his cock against her slick folds. "Beg for my cock, slut. Tell me how badly you need it..." He demands, teasing her hole with shallow thrusts that make her whimper and clench.

Niharika cries out, wiggling her hips desperately. "Please Neel, I need it! I need your big cock stuffed in my tight little cunt! Fuck me, ruin me for my husband! Make me cum on your dick!" She pleads shamelessly, too far gone in her lust to care about her wedding vows.

Satisfied with her begging, Neel slams his hips forward, burying himself to the hilt in one brutal thrust. Niharika screams in ecstasy, her walls gripping him like a vice as he starts to pound into her mercilessly.

Neel's hips piston in a relentless rhythm, his heavy balls slapping against Niharika's clit with every thrust. The wet, obscene sounds of flesh meeting flesh fill the room, mingling with Niharika's high-pitched moans and Neel's grunts of pleasure.

"Yes, yes, fuck me harder Neel! Ruin my cunt with your huge cock!" Niharika wails, meeting his thrusts eagerly. She braces herself on her elbows, pushing her hips back to take him even deeper, the head of his cock kissing her cervix with every stroke.

Neel reaches around to maul her bouncing tits, pinching and twisting her nipples roughly as he rails into her from behind. "Fuck, your pussy feels so good squeezing my dick... Gonna fill this cunt with my cum and seal it shut before your wedding night..."

Niharika's eyes roll back in her head, her tongue lolling out as she loses herself in the pleasure. "Ohhh, Neel, I'm gonna cum again! Fuck, I'm cumming!" She screams, her body convulsing as another powerful orgasm rips through her. Her pussy clamps down on Neel's cock, milking him for every drop of his seed.

The feel of her walls clamping down on him like a silken vise is too much for Neel. With a feral growl, he slams into her one last time, burying himself to the hilt as his cock erupts, painting her insides with thick ropes of his hot seed. "Take it all, you cum slut! Gonna breed this pussy and ruin it for anyone else!"

Niharika moans weakly, shuddering as she feels Neel's cum flooding her artificial cunt, sealing it shut just like he promised. As their orgasms subside, Neel slumps against her back, both of them panting heavily.

After a moment, Neel pulls out with a wet squelch, his cum dripping out of Niharika's well-fucked hole. "Fuck, that was intense..." He murmurs, giving her ass a final smack before standing up on shaky legs.

Niharika collapses onto the bed, her legs still trembling from the force of her climax. "Mmmm...you sure know how to give a girl a good seeing-to, Neel..." She purrs, basking in the afterglow. "But I should get cleaned up before the wedding rehearsal...wouldn't want anyone to suspect anything."

Neel chuckles, tucking himself back into his pants, zipping up and giving Niharika a roguish wink. "I don't think anyone would suspect a thing, love. Not unless they find my cum dripping out of your well-fucked cunt at the altar..." He jokes, eliciting a shocked gasp from Niharika.

"Neel!" She scolds, tossing a pillow at his head. "You can't say things like that! I'm getting married tomorrow!"

Neel catches the pillow, laughing. "Relax, I'm just messing with you. But in all seriousness, Niharika..." His expression sobers, his eyes softening as he gazes at her. "I'm glad we could reconnect like this, even if it's just one last hurrah before you tie the knot. I've always cared about you, you know."

Niharika's heart flutters at his words, a wistful smile playing on her lips. "I've always cared about you too, Neel. You'll always have a special place in my heart, no matter what."

She sits up, the sheet falling away to reveal her gorgeous, well-used body. Neel's eyes rake over her appreciatively, committing every curve to memory. "You'd better get going though," Niharika says softly. "I don't want you to miss the rehearsal dinner."

Neel nods, leaning down to press one last passionate kiss to her lips. "Take care of yourself, Niharika. And congratulations on your wedding. I hope you and John will be very happy together."

Niharika smiles softly, cupping Neel's cheek. "Thank you, Neel. For everything. For the memories, the laughs, the...other stuff." She giggles, her eyes sparkling with mischief. "I'll never forget you."

Neel grins, giving her one more quick peck before standing up. "I'll never forget you either, love. Now get cleaned up before you're late for your own wedding rehearsal!"

With a final wink, Neel grabs his clothes and heads for the door, pausing to take one last look at Niharika's glorious naked form sprawled across the bed. With a contented sigh, he slips out of the room, closing the door quietly.

Niharika lies back on the bed, her mind a whirlwind of emotions. She knows she made the right choice in marrying John, but Neel's passionate farewell has left her heart aching in a way she never expected. As she drifts off to sleep, she can't help but wonder if she'll ever feel this kind of raw, unbridled passion again....

# Chapter 23

As sunlight kissed Niharika's skin, she felt a flutter of excitement. The soft ringing of her phone interrupted her thoughts. It was her mother-in-law, Miss Sanjana.

"Hey, sweetheart! Are you awake?" Sanjana's voice was bubbling with enthusiasm.

"Yes, Mom, just now," Niharika replied, shaking off sleep.

"Get ready, dear! It's your big day! We're all waiting for you in the makeup room!" Sanjana urged, her excitement palpable.

Today was monumental; she was marrying John in a grand wedding attended by celebrities and prominent figures from across the country. The palace venue sparkled with elaborate floral arrangements and twinkling lights, setting a fairytale backdrop for the high-profile affair.

After a quick shower, Niharika poured herself a cup of coffee, the rich aroma grounding her as thoughts of the previous night with Neel lingered in her mind. She quickly shook off the guilt and slipped into a silk robe before heading to the makeup room.

Inside, her best friend Shalini, her bridesmaid, was already buzzing with energy. "Are you ready to become a stunning bride?" she teased, holding up a shimmering hairpiece.

"Ready as I'll ever be!" Niharika laughed, the anticipation rising in her chest.

As the makeup artist began her work, the transformation began. Foundation created a flawless canvas, and her hair was expertly curled into soft waves, cascading down her back. Niharika admired her reflection; her eyes sparkled with elegant makeup, and her lips glowed with a soft sheen. Finally, she slipped into her exquisite wedding gown-a strapless creation with intricate lace that flowed into a dramatic train.

"You look absolutely breathtaking!" Shalini exclaimed, capturing the moment on her phone.

Miss Sanjana entered, her eyes lighting up. "You're going to make John weak in the knees! Just remember, dear, happy wife, happy life!" she teased, a playful glint in her eye.

As they arrived at the venue, Niharika felt the electric atmosphere buzz with excitement. The palace was filled with well-known faces, from film stars to influential figures, all there to celebrate their union. Niharika felt a rush of emotions as she spotted John waiting at the altar, looking dapper in his tailored suit. During the ceremony, Niharika couldn't help but notice Neel's warm smile among the guests. Their eyes met briefly, and a swirl of feelings washed over her, but she quickly focused on John, who was grinning from ear to ear.

After exchanging vows and lighting the unity candle, the couple celebrated with family and friends at a lavish reception. Amidst the laughter and dancing, John leaned in close to Niharika. "I can't wait for our first night together," he whispered playfully. "Just remember, tradition is key!" His mischievous grin made her blush.

As the night wound down, Miss Sanjana caught up with Niharika. "Don't forget, tonight is special! Wear something traditional yet seductive," she encouraged, her eyes sparkling with motherly wisdom.

Niharika's heart raced as she thought about the outfit she had chosen-a stunning red and gold lehenga that hugged her curves, paired with intricate jewelry. The outfit was sensual yet elegant, reflecting her heritage beautifully. She styled her hair in a sophisticated bun adorned with fresh flowers, allowing a few strands to frame her face delicately.

As she prepared for the night, she held a glass of warm milk, a traditional gesture her mother-in-law had insisted on. "It's good for you, especially tonight," Sanjana teased, winking knowingly.

With a mix of excitement and nervousness, Niharika took a deep breath as she stepped into the softly lit suite where John awaited her. The atmosphere was thick with anticipation.

Just as she was about to enter, she felt a fleeting touch of guilt as thoughts of Neel crept back in. Shaking her head, she focused on the love she had for John.

When she finally opened the door, the sight of John in a relaxed yet dashing outfit made her heart flutter. "You look incredible," he said, his voice low and inviting.

Niharika felt the weight of the moment; this was a night that would define their future together. As they moved closer, the air crackled with suspense and desire. Would she be able to let go of her past and embrace this new beginning?

The night held countless possibilities, and as they embraced, she realized they were ready to face whatever came next-together. But as the door closed behind them, Niharika couldn't shake the feeling that this was just the beginning of a journey filled with unexpected twists and turns...

# Epilogue

As the night deepened, Niharika's heart raced with a mix of excitement and nervousness.

She knew John had been waiting for this moment, and she was ready to unleash her wild side. With a naughty smile, she offered him a glass of milk, leaving a bold lipstick mark as an invitation. John's eyes sparkled as he took a sip, matching her mark with a sensual smirk.

"At last," he purred, his voice thick with desire. "I've been craving this." He pulled her close, his hands roaming over her curves, and their lips met in a passionate kiss. Their tongues tangled, exploring each other's mouths, igniting a fire within. John's skilled hands found their way under her blouse, cupping her soft, perky boobs. Niharika's breath hitched, her nipples hardening at his touch.

Clothes were shed with eager haste, and Niharika stood before him, a vision of eroticism.

John's eyes devoured her, taking in her flawless body, her skin glowing in the soft light. "Oh, fuck, you're a gorgeous , my wifey ," he groaned, his voice husky with desire. He pulled her closer, his hands tracing her neck, leaving a trail of kisses as his erection grew to impressive proportions.

Niharika's eyes widened as she felt the size of his cock pressing against her, a stark contrast to her ex-boyfriend meager offerings. John's fingers danced along her wet pussy, teasing her with his massive girth. She moaned, her body craving the satisfaction only he could provide.

John signaled her to kneel, and as she did, he positioned himself, his cock pointing towards her mouth. Niharika, without hesitation, took him into her mouth,her enthusiasm matching his growing excitement,

His cock, engorged with desire, found its way into her mouth, a wet, warm haven. Niharika's lips, stretched to their limit, enveloped his shaft, her tongue darting out to tease the sensitive head. She sucked and slurped, her small hands stroking his length, her long hair, tied in a messy bun, creating a support against the wall, a barrier between her and the world outside their twisted game.

John's eyes darkened with desire as he watched her, his cock throbbing in her mouth. He guided her head, his hands gently cupping her cheeks, as she took him deeper, her throat working in perfect rhythm. He pre-cummed, the taste of his excitement filling her mouth, and she swallowed, eager for more.

John pulled her up, his hands resting on her hips, and led her to the bed. He positioned her on all fours, her ass high in the air, and entered her from behind. His cock slid into her pussy, stretching her, and he began to thrust, his balls slapping against her clenching ass. Niharika's eyes closed, her body adjusting to the intense pleasure.

As they moved in perfect sync, Niharika's guilt began to surface. She wanted to reveal her secret, to free herself from the burden. "John, I need to tell you something," she whispered, her voice trembling. "I can't hide it anymore." John, sensing her distress, stopped, his eyes filled with concern. "What is it, my love?" he asked gently.

Niharika took a deep breath and revealed her truth. She told him about her past, she removed her artificial vagina revealing her small cock to him.

John's eyes widened, but his expression remained compassionate. "I understand, my dear," he said, his voice soft and reassuring. "Let's make this even more intimate."

He guided her to the edge of the bed, her legs spread wide, and positioned himself between her thighs. Niharika's eyes widened as she saw the size of her cock, a stark contrast to John's massive member. He guided her cock into his mouth, his lips stretching to accommodate her girth. She moaned, her hands gripping the sheets, as he sucked and licked, bringing her to the brink of orgasm.

John's skilled fingers found her spot, his touch sending shivers down her spine. He rubbed and circled, his mouth never leaving her cock, as she felt the dual pleasure building.

Niharika's body trembled, her eyes closing in ecstasy, as she came in his mouth, her cock pulsating with pleasure.

John, not done yet, instructed her to lie on her back, her bum cheeks spread wide. He positioned himself between her thighs, his cock poised at her entrance of heaven . He entered her slowly, his eyes locked with hers, and she gasped, feeling the stretch of his massive girth.

He began to thrust, his cock filling her completely, and she moaned,John's hands cupped her ass, his fingers tracing her crack, as he pounded into her. Niharika's eyes rolled back, her body surrendering to the intense pleasure.

They moved together, their bodies synchronized, their moans filling the room. Niharika's hole throbbed, her cock twitching with each thrust, as John's cock filled her anus, stretching her beyond belief. They reached their climax together, their bodies shaking, their moans merging into a symphony of passion.

John's cum flooded her asshole, his cock pulsating as he came, and she cried out, her orgasm rippling through her body. They lay there, exhausted yet satisfied, their breath mingling. Niharika turned her head, her eyes meeting John's, and they shared a knowing smile, a bond strengthened by their intimate connection.

As the night wore on, they explored more positions, their bodies moving in perfect harmony. John and Niharika's marriage was a testament to their unyielding love, a union that transcended societal norms.